"You're a beautiful woman, Megan," Josh said, his hands caressing her back and shoulders.

When she opened her eyes, Josh glimpsed the sultry promise of her sensual nature. His fingers flexed, pressing into her satiny flesh, and he felt his body respond.

"Thank you," Megan said. "You have great hands. You must have been a masseur in another life."

Josh held his breath for a moment. "A man could drown in you."

"I'd save him," she whispered.

He smiled then, the slow, erotic smile that had the power to shake her to the core and level her defenses. "You would, wouldn't you?"

She nodded. "My sister the shrink says I have the classic caretaker personality. It's my destiny."

He gave her a look that made her insides sizzle. "Does that mean you plan to take care of me?"

She laughed. "If the need arises. But would you really ever let anyone care about you that way?"

His gaze narrowed speculatively. "I might be persuaded, but only under the right circumstances." He anchored their hips together with one hand and slid the other up her spine to her neck. The feel of her warm, fragrant skin and the silken weight of her thick auburn curls tortured his senses and tested his self-control.

"This is a dangerous game we're playing, Joshua Wyatt," she said quietly.

He smiled, knowing it was true. "You're a temptation I didn't anticipate. . . ."

WHAT ARE *LOVESWEPT* ROMANCES?

They are stories of true romance and touching emotion. We believe those two very important ingredients are constants in our highly sensual and very believable stories in the *LOVESWEPT* line. Our goal is to give you, the reader, stories of consistently high quality that may sometimes make you laugh, sometimes make you cry, but are always fresh and creative and contain many delightful surprises within their pages.

Most romance fans read an enormous number of books. Those they truly love, they keep. Others may be traded with friends and soon forgotten. We hope that each *LOVESWEPT* romance will be a treasure—a "keeper." We will always try to publish

LOVE STORIES YOU'LL NEVER FORGET BY AUTHORS YOU'LL ALWAYS REMEMBER

The Editors

Laura Taylor
Promises

BANTAM BOOKS
NEW YORK · TORONTO · LONDON · SYDNEY · AUCKLAND

PROMISES

A Bantam Book / February 1992

If you would be interested in receiving protective vinyl
covers for your Loveswept books, please write to this address
for information:

Loveswept
Bantam Books
P.O. Box 985
Hicksville, NY 11802

ISBN 0-553-44224-4

Published simultaneously in the United States and Canada

Bantam Books are published by Bantam Books, a division
of Bantam Doubleday Dell Publishing Group, Inc. Its trademark, consisting of the words "Bantam Books" and the
portrayal of a rooster, is Registered in U.S. Patent and
Trademark Office and in other countries. Marca Registrada.
Bantam Books, 666 Fifth Avenue, New York, New York 10103.

PRINTED IN THE UNITED STATES OF AMERICA

OPM   0 9 8 7 6 5 4 3 2 1

To Beth de Guzman and Nita Taublib,
two special friends

One

Joshua Wyatt made sure his face concealed his mixed emotions as he walked into the foyer of the converted Victorian-style mansion housing Primrose Preschool.

Maryville, Alabama, was the last place he wanted to be, but he knew he couldn't avoid a meeting with the executor of the estate of the late Charles Stanton any longer.

Shrugging out of his raincoat, Josh studied the long-legged, auburn-haired woman sprawled on her stomach on the playroom floor. He watched her reach out and tweak the nose of one of a dozen or so laughing preschoolers gathered on the floor around her. She left her mark, a smudge of fluorescent orange finger paint.

The recipient of the paint giggled with delight and returned the favor. Several other small children joined the fray. The decibel level of the noise in the room immediately rose, drowning out the late-afternoon thunderstorm raging outside.

Despite the ironfisted control Josh instinctively exercised over himself and his world, desire sparked to life deep inside him as the woman on the floor tried to escape the squealing assault. She twisted and turned as the children surged over her and gleefully daubed paint on any part of her writhing body they could reach.

The oversized T-shirt she wore bunched around her midriff, revealing a miniscule waist, rounded fanny, and shapely hips. Uninhibited laughter spilled from her as she shielded her face with her hands, rolled onto her back, and dramatically pleaded for a reprieve.

Josh narrowed his blue eyes. The abundance of the woman's hourglass figure—poorly concealed beneath her T-shirt and the snug leggings that encased her endless legs—distracted him.

Angry with himself for reacting to her, but even angrier with her for arousing him, he breathed an oath. Josh wrenched his thoughts back to the purpose of his trip and reminded himself that he didn't need any distractions, not even one as sumptuous as the sensual creature on the floor.

One by one, the giggling children noticed him, and big-eyed with curiosity, they all fell silent.

Quickly registering the shift in the attention of her charges and the sudden quiet of the room, Megan Montgomery lifted her head and peered at their visitor. A mixture of surprise, dismay, and then recognition widened her large hazel eyes.

Flushing, she scrambled to her feet, tugging her shirt down as she moved forward. "Pardon the paint, and welcome to Primrose—"

Seduced anew by the sultry sound of her voice, Josh interrupted her. "I'm looking for Megan Montgomery."

His low, cold voice sent chill bumps skittering across her skin and up her spine. Megan shivered, but she wasn't the kind of woman who backed away from adversity. "I'm Megan, and you're Joshua Wyatt. I've been expecting you."

He gave her a hard, speculative look. Although he wondered how she'd identified him with such ease, he first grappled with his surprise that the executor of Charles Stanton's estate was a spirited young woman with a face and body that provoked achingly lustful cravings.

"*You're* Megan Montgomery?"

She nodded, amusement shining in her eyes. "You expected someone older, didn't you?"

Guarded as always, Josh conceded, "Perhaps."

She grinned. "Don't feel alone. Most everyone did, especially here in Maryville." She glanced down at the child who seemed intent on attaching himself to her right thigh. "Excuse me a moment." Placing a gentle hand on the little boy's shoulder, she leaned over. "What's wrong, Teddy?"

"Did he come to steal us?"

Megan frowned and dropped to her knees, her curly auburn mane cascading halfway down her back as she took the child's hands in her own and gave him her full attention.

"Of course not, Teddy. I wouldn't let anyone steal you, so you don't have a thing to worry about." She hugged him and then pressed a kiss to his furrowed brow. "I'm putting you in charge today. Will you lead everyone into the kitchen for a juice break? And tell Miss Caroline that I'll be busy for a while."

Teddy, his attention still captured by the intimidating-looking man towering over Megan, said, "Yes, ma'am," before reluctantly slipping away.

Smiling, Megan got to her feet. "Sorry about that. Teddy's mother has spent a lot of time recently warning him about strangers. Unfortunately, he now thinks everyone wants to kidnap him."

Josh recalled the isolation of his own childhood, but he made certain his expression remained impassive. "The world's a tough place."

"It can be," she agreed softly, "but paranoia's not the answer. I'm sure there's a happy medium."

"We need to talk."

She laughed, not in the least put off by his bluntness. "I totally agree. I can't tell you how glad I am to finally meet you, Josh." Glancing down at herself, Megan grimaced. "If you'll give me a couple of minutes, I'll get cleaned up. The staff will take care of the children until their parents come to collect them."

Josh snagged her wrist as she began to move past him. "Don't bother. Just tell me why Stanton picked you to handle his estate."

Startled by his touch and his manner, Megan felt the pulse points in her body start to flutter. She looked up at him, her gaze fixed on the harshly chiseled contours of his rugged face.

Though she'd seen several photographs of Josh Wyatt over the years, she realized that the force of his masculinity couldn't be fully measured or appreciated without person-to-person contact.

She knew now that the photos had also failed to capture the dangerous glint in his eyes and the flinty hardness of his personality. Megan experienced a sensual tug low in her belly at the sudden realization that he would, no doubt, be an extremely demanding lover.

She exhaled shakily, startled that her thoughts had strayed to such an unexpected arena. Refocusing on the face of the man studying her with obvious sexual interest, she realized that she didn't mind his blunt perusal. She didn't mind it at all. He stirred something to life inside her that she hadn't ever felt before.

Megan already knew that Josh Wyatt was no stranger to the less refined side of life. According to the investigative reports Charles Stanton had shown her, the bastard grandson of the late patriarch of Maryville, Alabama, had grown up angry, wild, and rebellious. Despite all that, he'd achieved success in the travel industry, and perhaps, she speculated, because of all that, he had a reputation as an aggressive and very tough businessman.

He was neither pretty nor polished, despite the affluence reflected in his black linen trousers, a shirt of pale gray silk, the silver Rolex fastened at his wrist, and the handmade leather loafers she'd noticed from her vantage point on the floor.

Josh Wyatt wasn't like any man she'd ever met, she realized. He looked intimidating, powerful, and dangerous, and she suddenly knew that he was all those things, and perhaps even more.

His jet-black hair, which he wore slightly longer than was fashionable, dark complexion, and strong facial features confirmed his bold approach to life and a distinct disdain for weakness in others. His blue eyes announced defiance and a worldliness that proclaimed an early loss of innocence.

Her single regret at the moment was that the startling blue of his eyes lacked even a hint of warmth. Instead, they reminded her of an arctic tundra. Megan decided that his patience was limited, his judgments utterly final.

"I really need to change." She smiled and eased free of him, but she froze in midstride when he lifted his hand to her face.

He cupped the side of her head with his big hand, his thumb whisking back and forth across her cheek. "Paint," he observed succinctly as heat seared her flushed skin.

Megan's smile faded. Confusion darkened her hazel eyes to a rich brown. "Thank you," she whispered, her heart thudding rapidly at the unexpected gentleness of his touch.

"You're welcome."

Mindful of the audience of little people peering at them from the open kitchen door down the hall, she steadied herself by sheer force of will. "I live upstairs. If you'd like, you can wait in the library while I change clothes."

Josh lowered his hand, his expression calculating. Unsettled by his touch, Megan gathered her scattered wits and moved out of reach.

"I still want to know why you're the executor of the Stanton estate."

Tenderly recalling her former neighbor, she paused at the bottom of a curved oak staircase. "Charles insisted, I'm afraid. That's not a problem, is it?"

"Only if you make it one," he answered, his tone terse as he followed her up a flight of stairs to the second story of the sprawling mansion.

"I won't give you a speck of trouble," she promised lightly as she paused on the landing. "I'm too glad you're finally here. The library's the second door on your right. Make yourself comfortable. If you'd like something to drink, you'll find refreshments in the bar. I'll be right back."

Josh didn't budge. Implacable and determined, he pressed for an answer. "Why?"

Megan paused at her bedroom door, the coiled tension emanating from Josh Wyatt beginning to encompass her, too. He reminded her of a rattler poised to strike. His defensiveness eroded her pleasure at his arrival.

"Why what?" she asked very quietly, and very stubbornly.

"Why are you the executor of the will of an old man who was three times your age?"

His persistent pursuit of the subject, not to mention his unconcealed impatience, grated on her nerves. Equally impatient now, Megan retorted, "That's what friends do for one another, Josh, but perhaps you don't have the kind of friends who can be trusted with such important tasks."

Satisfied that she'd given him something to

ponder when she saw the surprise that flitted across his face, she turned and walked into her bedroom. After closing and locking the door, Megan hurriedly shed her clothes, scrubbed the washable paint from her face and arms, donned a floor-length silk caftan, and then ran a brush through her tangled hair.

She didn't let herself dwell on Josh's overt hostility or his suspicious nature. Given what she knew about him, she didn't feel the need to criticize him. Nor did she let herself devote more than a few seconds to her shocking response to him or his ability to provoke her Irish temper.

Instead, she concentrated on how she would keep the promise she'd made to Charles Stanton prior to his death. Come hell or high water, Megan silently vowed, she would help Josh discover his heritage. She knew she couldn't alter his past, but she could show him that he now had a home he could call his own.

Josh heard Megan enter the library, but he didn't abandon his position in front of the French doors that led out onto the balcony.

"Most of the children are collected by their parents by six," she told him as the telltale sounds of energetic children drifted upward from the lower level. "It should be peaceful around here fairly soon."

He glanced at her, noting her poise as she settled into a nearby chair. "The rain's stopped," he observed, his voice deceptively even.

"That's a relief. With the play yard on the verge

of turning into a pond, we've had to devise new ways to entertain the kids." She smiled. "It takes a bit of imagination."

"I wouldn't know." Josh finally turned and faced her. "Do you expect us to be friends?"

"I would hope that we aren't enemies, but I suspect everything depends on just how bull-headed you intend to be."

He hadn't expected a flower of Southern womanhood to have such a tart tongue or volatile temper. His imagination unexpectedly produced a mental image of Megan sprawled naked, exposed, and pliant beneath him. Caught off guard, he clenched his fists and remarked, "You must be like satin-covered dynamite in bed."

I can play this game, too, Joshua Wyatt. "And you're probably pure dynamite, but that has nothing whatever to do with the issue at hand."

"Why do you give a damn about what some old man wanted?"

"I told you, he was my friend."

Josh gave her a skeptical look. "What's in it for you, Megan?"

"A lot of aggravation," she said dryly, thinking of all the correspondence and requests for contact made by the estate's lawyer that Josh had ignored since Stanton's death early the previous year. She couldn't help wondering if the letter she finally wrote to him five weeks before had prompted his visit.

"Then why do it?"

"Because I loved him," she admitted. "And because I made a promise."

He suddenly loathed the idea that Megan

Montgomery could care about a manipulative old man, but he didn't bother to ask himself why. "And you always keep your promises?"

"Well, of course. Don't you?"

"When I make them."

She watched him closely, taking in his cynical expression and the controlled strength of his powerful body as he crossed the room. Joshua Wyatt moved like a predator intent on a kill.

Megan sighed softly when he paused in front of the built-in mahogany bar situated in the center of a wall populated by a vast collection of books. A sudden spurt of insight prompted her to comment. "You don't make many promises, do you?"

"Rarely."

"You don't trust people, do you?"

"Rarely," he bit out a second time as he splashed cognac from a crystal decanter into a snifter, then lounged against the mahogany bar. "Your letter *aroused* my curiosity."

She ignored his suggestive tone of voice. "Had I known, I would've written sooner."

Megan got to her feet and made her way across the room, the silk of her caftan softly rustling against her body with each step she took. After retrieving an already-open bottle of wine from the bar's refrigerator, she poured a small amount of Chardonnay into a goblet. She glanced at him before taking a sip. "This is really ridiculous, Josh. We're on the same side."

"Was he your lover?" he demanded, the sound of rustling silk still echoing in his ears and the image of the fabric making love to her body burning in his mind.

Megan almost dropped her drink. Her composure flew out the window. "Was he *what*?"

"Did you sleep with him?"

"He was like a grandfather to me!" she exclaimed, shocked. "How utterly perverse. How could you even think such a thing?"

"It happens," he observed blandly as the fragrance of wild lilacs teased his senses.

"Perhaps in your world, but not in mine, so get your mind out of the gutter and listen very carefully, because I'll say this only once. Charles Stanton was my neighbor and my friend. He was also an extremely lonely old man who paid dearly for his prideful ways. When he prevented your parents from marrying, his only child drank himself into an early grave, and Charles felt he'd deprived you of a father and a real family. By the time he tried to rectify a thirty-five-year-old mistake in judgment, it was too late. You refused to see him. As much as he understood your rejection, it still hurt him."

"Are you a beneficiary?" Josh pressed.

Exasperated with him, Megan exhaled heavily. "*You* are the sole beneficiary."

"You must be disappointed."

"I don't think I've ever met anyone quite so cynical. I feel sorry for you."

A muscle jumped in his cheek. He slammed his snifter onto the bar and then wrenched the goblet she held from her hand. White wine sloshed across her fingers. Before Megan could step back, Josh seized her upper arms and jerked her against him.

"Save your pity. It's a wasted emotion, and it

accomplishes nothing. The only valuable com-modity in this world is power."

"But I do pity you, Josh," she countered in a scathing tone, "because I think *any* emotion is wasted on you."

"How dare you," he seethed, his eyes like shards of ice. "How *dare* you."

"I dare because I promised to dare. And I keep my promises. No matter what you seem to think, he loved you, Josh. As proof of his love and his regret for the mistakes he made, he left you everything he owned, everything he spent a lifetime creating and nurturing."

"Damn you!"

She glared at him, her emotions rattled and her senses in chaos as she absorbed his seductive heat, his unyielding torso, and his fury. She heard him whisper, "Damn you!" once again, but this time the words reminded her of a reluctant caress.

Megan stared up at him, her heart tripping wildly in her chest. Heat unexpectedly pooled low in her abdomen. She felt her cheeks flush, her eyes widen in disbelief.

"Josh," she whispered gently. "I know this is hard for you." Lifting her hands, she pressed them against his broad chest. She indulged in-stinct, not common sense, as she flexed her fin-gers against the rippling muscles beneath his shirt.

A sizzling current rose up between them. Megan held her breath.

He tightened his grip on her, his fingers digging into her upper arms as he rejected the concept that Charles Stanton was capable of anything but manipulation and cruelty. He couldn't, however, reject or ignore the woman he held.

Megan saw a hint of violence in his expression. Oddly, she felt no fear, only desire tangled up with compassion.

"I'm hard for you," he muttered in a low voice that thoroughly ravaged her composure.

She flinched. "You're being crude. This situation is difficult enough as it is."

"I'm being honest."

Megan paled, but she held perfectly still and kept her eyes on Josh's stormy countenance. He immediately thwarted her attempt at indifference when he slid his hands down her body, seized her hips, and pulled her between his muscled thighs. When she tensed, he chalked up a small victory.

"How much do you know about me?" he demanded, her wild lilac scent engulfing him yet again.

"Enough," she admitted cautiously. "But this isn't about you and me. This isn't about us." Her knees threatened to buckle, but she fought the urge to give in to the desire and raw emotion charging through her bloodstream.

This shouldn't be happening, she reminded herself harshly. You have a job to do, and a promise to keep.

"I want you, Megan Montgomery."

Two

Josh lowered his lips to hers and took, no, *demanded*, repayment for her knowledge of him and her denial of the explosive chemistry swirling around them. He invaded her mouth, intent on satisfying the harsh ache that throbbed within his body and enflamed his senses.

Thoroughly stunned, Megan didn't move. But neither did she participate. She simply stood there, assaulted by the inferno that was his body, tortured by the musky smell of his skin, and stunned by the experienced sweep of his tongue as he seduced her senses.

Against her will, desire exploded within her. Josh aroused a hunger in her, an almost voracious hunger, for feelings and experiences her muddled brain couldn't even begin to define.

She stiffened finally, fighting his power, his beckoning heat, and the blatant arousal pressing against her lower abdomen, branding her, shattering the remnants of her composure. She was on the verge of abandoning every self-protective instinct she possessed as need rampaged within her.

Josh reluctantly released her mouth, but only after her resistance had waned. He smiled then, a slow, seductive, and thoroughly compelling smile that sent a tremor through her soul. "This *is* about us, Megan."

Shaken, she insisted breathlessly, "There is no *us*."

"Don't lie to yourself."

Color filled her face. "I'm not a part of your inheritance. You're here to assume control of an estate that impacts an entire community, and I also hope you're here to fill in parts of your life that are incomplete."

"There's nothing incomplete about my life."

His denial didn't ring true, and she sensed that she'd discovered a fissure in an otherwise-impenetrable wall of defense.

"Isn't there?" Megan asked. "Charles is dead, so whatever happens now is up to you. He can't hurt you ever again, but if you let history repeat itself, if you allow your bitterness and resentment to consume you, then you'll be just as lonely as he was. Please don't blind yourself to the real wealth of his estate. You have a chance now to explore your heritage, as well as an opportunity to experience a sense of belonging I suspect you've never enjoyed. Can't we declare a truce and work together, or are you going to wallow in self-pity for the rest of your life because you entered the world as the bastard grandson of Charles Stanton?"

Josh stiffened. Those people who knew the circumstances of his birth invariably avoided the subject. Shamed and isolated by his bastard status as a child, and noncommittal about it as an adult, he was torn between cursing Megan for her insight where he was concerned and applauding her nerve. In the end he did neither.

Instead he agreed. "You're right, Megan. I am a bastard, a coldhearted bastard. Just ask anyone who's ever done business with me. I also don't give a damn about Charles Stanton or what he wanted. Nor do I feel the need to belong in some one-horse town that apparently idolizes a person I loathe. I have a life in St. Louis, so please explain to me what I need with some old man's guilt-induced largess. I came to Maryville to renounce the Stanton estate, and that's exactly what I intend to do. Any questions?"

Megan managed to conceal her shock. Exhaling softly, she tugged free of Josh and walked to the balcony doors, her hands clasped in front of her, her head bowed as she tried to determine her next move. Her heart thundered deafeningly in her ears as she struggled to set aside her dismay.

Turning to face him a few moments later, she said, "It's going to take some time to have all the paperwork prepared."

"My time is my own."

"Then perhaps you'd like a guided tour of what you're rejecting while the attorney assembles the necessary documents."

Josh shrugged, his expression unreadable.

"Regardless of your decision, you'll also need to sort through Charles's diaries and personal papers."

"Burn them."

She remained stoic. "Then there's Stanton House."

"His home?"

She nodded.

"I don't want it."

Megan flinched, aware she couldn't, and wouldn't, accept his dismissal of the symbols of Charles Stanton's life and goals. She firmly believed that the past had a place in the present and the future.

"Would you like to stay for supper?" she asked. "It won't be fancy, but we still have several things we need to discuss."

When Josh frowned in response to her invitation, Megan held her breath and forced herself to wait patiently for his reply. So much depended on his willingness to linger in Maryville. Shifting uncomfortably, she silently endured his lengthy silence and probing gaze, despite the fact that the waiting wore thin nerves already stretched to the limit.

When she couldn't take it any longer, she asked, "Josh, will you stay?"

"Why?"

"I thought you might be hungry."

He gave her a hot look that made her heart stop beating. She hastily pointed out, "I'm not talking about sex. I'm simply talking about two adults sharing a meal. That's all."

"Why did you lie to me?"

"Did I?" she asked.

"Don't be coy, Megan. It doesn't suit you."

"I wrote to you because I was desperate. The lawyer had spent nearly a year trying to get you down here, and you wouldn't even answer his letters. You forced my hand. I'm certain you would've done the same thing if you found yourself in my situation."

Josh ignored her observation. "Your letter implied that I was jeopardizing the well-being of an entire community, but Maryville is obviously a prosperous place."

"I was trying to provoke your conscience."

"At least be honest about your motives. You were trying to shame me into a response."

She nodded, worry consuming her confidence. "You're right. I hoped that the same humanitarian instincts your grandfather had were a part of your character, too."

"I've been told I don't have a conscience. You shouldn't ever forget that, because it's probably true."

"I don't believe it for a minute."

"Then you're a fool."

"Maybe I am, but you're here, aren't you? So I'm not as big a fool as you'd like to think."

"Don't ever cast me in the same mold as Charles Stanton. I'm nothing like him."

"You not only resemble him, you sound like him, and you have many of his mannerisms and character traits." Megan abandoned all caution and kept talking, despite the storm brewing in Josh's cold eyes. "He had a conscience, Josh, and he *was* considered something of a humanitarian. You can believe whatever you want about your grandfather, but I saw proof of his generosity and kindness. Despite his pride, despite his intransigence on some issues, and perhaps because of the guilt he felt at failing you, he cared about people. I'm certain you care, too, but you're too stubborn to admit it to me or anyone else."

"Don't ever speculate about my motives or my character. As for Stanton, he cared about himself and the control he exercised over other people's lives."

"A man who didn't care would've trashed my letter, but you didn't."

"You're on thin ice, Megan."

Tired of their sniping, she asked, "Could we not argue?"

He moved toward her, his intent shielded behind his impassive features. He paused less than a foot away from her. Megan didn't step back. Instead, she absorbed the impact of Josh's gaze on her.

"As I said, Megan, my time is my own, but don't ever get the idea that my patience is limitless. It's not. I don't appreciate being lied to, and I won't be manipulated, so think carefully about your tactics where I'm concerned."

"My motives were, and are, honorable," she protested.

"Your motives," he countered harshly, "are highly suspect, especially from my perspective."

She closed the space that separated them, reached out and placed her hand on his forearm. "No one wants to hurt you, Josh, least of all me. Even if you can't find it in your heart to give Charles or yourself a chance, please give the people of Maryville a chance. They deserve it." So do you, she thought. So do you.

"No commitments, Megan. That's not my style."

Lifting her hand, she pressed her palm against the side of his face. His warmth and tension seeped into her skin, and she forced herself to quell the urge to comfort him. She sensed he wouldn't welcome the compassion she felt for him. "Don't be angry. It won't accomplish anything."

He resisted her gentleness, despite how inviting if felt. "Then don't try to seduce me for the wrong reasons. You'll fail. I cut my teeth on the games you're playing. I'm a master at them, Megan Montgomery, so consider yourself fully warned."

She smiled, knowing her eyes twinkled with renewed spirit. "I won't have to seduce you, because the people of Maryville will do it for me."

He took her hand, guided it to his lips, and used the tip of his tongue to make his mark in the center of her palm. He kept his gaze on her face the entire time, noting her breathlessness when he nipped the plump ridge of flesh at the base of her thumb.

When Megan shuddered, Josh felt a surge of satisfaction that he could arouse her so swiftly. Her reaction increased his confidence that she would be his equal as a lover.

"You're playing with fire," he observed. "But you already know that, don't you?"

Megan found her voice after several moments of diligent searching. "You have every intention of trying to seduce me."

"Are you asking me, or are you telling me?" he pressed, his voice so low, so rife with seductive appeal, that he sent a shaft of fear through Megan.

"I'm not sure," she finally whispered.

He smiled then, that same slow, steamy smile that made her insides tremble. "Why wouldn't I make every effort to seduce you, especially given the chemistry between us?"

She studied him for a long moment. "You wouldn't use me that way, Josh. It's not in you to hurt me."

"You're a trusting thing, aren't you?" he mused.

She nodded. "When it's warranted. You may have mastered survival and manipulation, but you aren't a cruel man. I also think you're smart enough to realize that while I may be impetuous, perhaps even short-tempered, I am not a fool."

He released her hand and stepped away from her. "Neither am I, Megan Montgomery. Neither am I."

Megan closed her hands into fists and pressed them to her sides, but the sensation caused by the feel of his sensual tongue, his lips, and his nipping teeth refused to retreat from her consciousness.

While Josh retrieved his snifter of brandy,

Megan mentally pulled herself together. Despite her certainty that he wouldn't hurt her or use her, she seriously doubted her own ability to remain emotionally aloof. Joshua Wyatt drew her to him like the proverbial moth in search of a deadly flame.

The only man she'd ever loved had been like her father—steady, easygoing, and never afraid to share a laugh or offer consolation. Until this moment Megan had believed that she wanted to find another man cut from the same cloth. Now, she wasn't so sure.

A soft sigh escaped her, but she squared her slender shoulders and produced a smile. "Which would you prefer? Cold seafood salad or some leftover fried chicken?"

He smiled, the first spontaneous smile he'd displayed since his arrival. "How about both? I haven't had time to eat today," he confessed.

Pleasure ignited within her when she glimpsed a hint of boyish innocence in the depths of his blue eyes. Megan sensed that she was seeing a side of Josh he rarely revealed to the world.

"You're in luck," she told him, striving for a casual tone of voice as they left the library and walked down the hallway to the kitchen. "My mother bombards me with food on a regular basis, so I've got plenty in the fridge. After living on my own after all these years, I still haven't convinced Mom that I eat well-balanced meals."

Josh gave her a thorough visual inspection as he slid onto a stool at the bar that separated the kitchen from a small dining alcove. "You look extremely well balanced to me."

She didn't miss the innuendo in his voice, but she laughed and wagged a warning with her finger. "Be nice, or you won't get fed."

Under Josh's observant gaze Megan assembled plates, cutlery, napkins, and two glasses of iced tea. She then arranged a buffet of leftovers on the kitchen countertop.

"If you'd like, we can take our trays out to the gazebo."

"The rain may start up again."

She smiled. "I'll tell you a secret. I love the rain. It tidies up the world. Besides, the gazebo is glass-enclosed, and the path to it is sheltered. It's peaceful out there, even in the middle of a storm."

Later, after dining in relative silence, Josh leaned back in his chair and studied Megan's relaxed features as she sipped her iced tea. They sat opposite each other, the darkness surrounding them like a cocoon. The only illumination in the gazebo came from the dim light of a half-dozen chunky candles positioned in the center of the wrought-iron table.

Adept at evaluating people, Josh now knew that his suspicion of Megan was unfounded, despite the fact that she'd stretched the truth in her letter to him. Sensitive, candid, sensual, unguarded, and even somewhat innocent, she lacked the hard shell of calculating worldliness the majority of his female acquaintances possessed.

He liked her, he realized. He liked the fact that

she spoke her mind, even if he didn't agree with her. And she was right that he wouldn't take advantage of her, despite the arousal he experienced every time he glanced at her.

"You're very quiet. What are you thinking about?"

He tilted his head to one side and gave her a thoughtful look. "Misconceptions."

"I don't understand."

"My misconception about Southern women. I always thought they were fluffy and lacked substance."

"We're people, for goodness sake, not cotton balls!"

He chuckled. "I know that now. In fact, now that I think about it, you've got the instincts of a street fighter."

She gave him a dubious look. "I guess that's a step up from being compared to a cotton ball, but you should know that the men of the South often describe their ladies as steel magnolias."

"Is that what your men call you?"

Megan grinned. "You mean that parade of guys lined up at my front door, even as we speak?" She shook her head, a teasing note still in her voice when she said, "It's my father's contention that the men of Maryville are put off by what he calls my headstrong nature. The rest of the family is more blunt. They all call me the resident bulldozer."

"Not known for your tact, huh?"

She flushed, recalling how she'd blundered through their first few minutes together. She'd been her usual unsubtle self. "It doesn't exactly take a mental giant to figure out why."

"The preschoolers obviously adore you."

"And I adore them."

"Why don't you have your own, Megan?"

"Children?"

He nodded, his expression intent.

"I'm waiting for the right man."

"Sounds like you've got a description of the guy."

"To a certain degree, I guess I do."

"Sir Galahad," he teased.

"Hardly. I don't believe in fantasies or fairy tales, Josh, but I do believe in the goodness of people and the rightness of loving."

"Quaint concept," he observed, his tone balanced between humor and sarcasm.

Megan remained unruffled. "Actually, it's very common."

"I'll take your word for it. Maryville appears to be a thriving place, so how come you haven't made it to the altar yet? No prospects?" he pressed.

She smiled briefly at his use of such an old-fashioned word. "My one *prospect* died in a hunting accident five years ago."

"I'm sorry."

Her gaze drifted to his clenched, white-knuckled fist. "Me, too. Tom was a good person. We grew up together, went off to school together. I guess we did nearly everything together." She looked back at Josh's face, her expression startlingly vulnerable. "At the time," she confided, "it seemed really odd to me that I didn't die when he did. Once I got over the shock of his death, I went through a period of anger."

"Anger?"

Megan nodded. "He abandoned me when he died, and it took me a while to forgive him."

Unsettled by her candor about such a painful event and by his own comprehension of what abandonment could do to a person, Josh shifted uncomfortably in his chair. "I didn't mean to intrude on your privacy."

"I don't mind talking about Tom. I finished grieving a long time ago. I have good memories of him. And," she added, "I really do believe that things happen for a reason, even if we don't always understand those reasons."

"How did you end up teaching preschool?"

"There's not much to tell. I was born in Maryville twenty-nine years ago, the third of seven children. My parents are terrific, and so are my sisters and brothers. Other than when I went away to college, I've always lived here." She shrugged as she absently stacked empty dishes and silverware onto the dinner tray. "I inherited Primrose Mansion from my great-aunt five-and-a-half years ago. I'd been teaching first grade at the local public school. Everything kind of fell into place after Charles suggested that I consider opening my own preschool."

Josh probed her guileless expression with a searching look before he asked, "Did Stanton help you financially?"

Their eyes met. Megan quelled her disappointment that Josh even felt the need to ask such a question.

"Charles contributed, but not monetarily. You might find this hard to believe, but he read to the children every afternoon for four years. They called him—" Emotion shattered her composure and tears welled in her eyes.

"Megan, I don't want to—"

She waved a hand in his direction. He fell silent as she blinked back her tears and cleared her throat.

"Let me finish, Josh. He was Grandpa Stanton to them, and they loved him. He spent time with them, not money. Primrose Mansion came with a generous trust fund from my great-aunt's will, as well as the stipulation that I was to use it for the benefit of the community and not simply as a personal residence."

He surged to his feet. "It's time for me to leave."

Startled by his abruptness, Megan said, "I guess it's my turn to apologize for being tactless. I didn't deliberately set out to remind you of the absence of family in your life, or to hurt you with an overview of what Charles was to other people. You should have been the recipient of his warmth and love. Unfortunately, you weren't."

Josh eyed her suspiciously. He also resisted the memory of all those times during his childhood when he longed for some small show of affection, some sense that he belonged, some indication that someone, somewhere, cared about him.

Resistance and reality collided within him. He moved around the table, willing a mask of indifference to freeze his features. Still, he couldn't completely block out the pain of having endured far too many years of emotional neglect.

Guided solely by instinct, Megan abandoned her chair and walked toward Josh. They paused within inches of each other. She trembled, and then very nearly wept when she glimpsed the resignation in his features. She suddenly realized that Joshua Wyatt had never been truly loved.

She reached out to him, even though she sensed that he might spurn her touch. Carefully pressing her hands against his chest, she searched for just the right thing to say as she felt the steady thudding of his heart and the warmth that emanated from his lean, hard body.

"Josh . . ." she began when he didn't turn away from her.

"Don't, Megan. I know what you're thinking, but you're wrong. I asked the questions, and you provided the answers. I can't and won't fault your honesty."

He trailed his fingertips down the side of her face, his senses registering the satiny texture of her fair skin and the thickness of the lashes that framed her large eyes. "I know you mean well, but there's no point to this. I live in the real world, and I've got a tough hide. That won't ever change."

"Don't be bitter."

"I'm not bitter. I am, however, a realist."

"You're missing so much," she whispered.

"A person doesn't miss what he's never had."

"I meant it before when I said that I didn't want to hurt you, Josh."

"You wear your heart on your sleeve, don't you?"

Stung by his comment, she tried to ease free of him, but he caught her by the shoulders and held her still.

"What you see is what you get," she said somewhat flippantly.

"What I see is a beautiful woman made vulnerable by her emotional attachment to the people she cares about."

"There's nothing wrong with caring and letting it show."

He smiled, but his eyes remained cold and hard. "It depends on your frame of reference. It's been my experience that most people want the trappings, not the real person."

"Then you know the wrong people. You can trust me."

"I'm not like you, Megan. Trust isn't an instinct with me. It's a part of my nature to weigh everything very carefully."

"Trust can be learned," she insisted.

"Trust is invariably abused." He searched her face and saw only sincerity. "If it's any consolation, Megan, I know you mean well."

"I do, but it doesn't seem to matter."

He released his hold on her, despite his urgent desire to draw her even closer and lose himself in her warmth and sensitivity. "Thanks for dinner. I enjoyed it."

Megan felt the harsh bite of Josh's dismissal, but she refused to give in to the negative feeling. "I'll walk you out to your car."

Three

Megan accompanied Josh to the foyer, where he collected his raincoat. The scent of a newly laundered world and the humid night air merged to form an almost tangible embrace as they stepped outside. Pausing at the bottom of the front steps, they faced each other under the muted front-porch light.

"You're really going to walk away from all of it, aren't you?" she finally asked.

He nodded, his expression resolute.

Megan extended her hand. Several keys attached to a woven rawhide key ring rested in her open palm. "These belong to you, Josh. The large silver key opens the front door of Stanton House. Other than the housekeeper, and me, of course, no one's been in the house since Charles died. You'll find everything in order."

He ground his teeth together, fury sweeping

forcefully through him. "You haven't heard a damn thing I've said, have you?"

"On the contrary. I've listened very carefully to everything you've said. I've also listened to what you haven't said. An intelligent man would ascertain the true extent of what he's rejecting, not just take a tour of the local countryside. I believe you're an intelligent man, Josh. Besides, you'll need a place to sleep at night. Why stay in a motel when you can be comfortable in a home that you own?"

"Back off, Megan."

"I can't," she said softly, despite the whiplash sting of his words.

"Your family's wrong about you. They should compare you to a war zone, not a bulldozer."

She grabbed his arm when he started to walk away. "Josh, there's no time for subtlety."

He exhaled, the sound harsh in the stillness of the night. "I've agreed to remain for a few days, but I meant it when I told you that I wouldn't let you manipulate me."

"Where are you staying?" Megan asked, retreating from the anger she had just induced. Dealing with Josh Wyatt was like trying to navigate a swaying tightrope with her feet encased in blocks of cement.

"At the Inn," he said, referring to a bed-and-breakfast establishment on the outskirts of Maryville.

"It's very nice, but you probably knew that before you arrived."

He worked at not smiling at her quicksilver

topic changes. "Being in the travel business gives me an edge."

"Shall we get started on your tour in the morning?" she asked.

Still somewhat wary of her change of tactics and subdued manner, Josh nodded. While he respected Megan's certainty of purpose, he refused to engage in a struggle over his decision regarding the Stanton estate.

"I'll pick you up around nine tomorrow morning," he said. "But understand me clearly this time, Megan. If you cross the line again, I'm gone. You'll be forced to deal with my lawyers."

She knew by his tone and his expression that he was serious. "You win, Josh, even though I think you're making a mistake." She hesitated for a moment as she searched his face. Frustration and defeat gnawed at her, but she said simply, "Good night," before turning away from him.

"Megan?"

She paused and looked back at him. "Yes?"

"I know I'm going to regret asking, but what's wrong now?"

"Nothing. I'm just tired. It's been a long day."

He moved closer. "Don't lie to me, Megan. You've got something on your mind, so why don't you just spit it out?"

"Trust me, you don't want to hear it."

He lifted her chin with his fingertips and forced her to look at him. When he saw the tears welling in her eyes, his common sense disappeared. Urging her forward, he smoothed his hands down her narrow back as he gathered her against him.

Megan sighed heavily. Josh recognized the sound as an echo of her defeat. He warned himself of the danger of allowing emotion, even one as innocent as compassion, to displace his pragmatic way of handling the world, but he quickly dismissed the warning.

After a brief mental debate she hesitantly slipped her arms around his waist. Relaxing against him, she savored the sense of well-being she found in his sturdiness and warmth. Josh's fingertips skimmed lightly back and forth across the small of her back and then up and down her spine. The tension of trying to persuade him to be less judgmental about the past started to seep from her body.

Instead of rejecting Megan's vulnerability, Josh found himself trusting a fledgling instinct that encouraged tenderness. Despite his habit of shutting himself off from the emotional needs of the women who had come and gone in his life, he realized he couldn't abandon Megan or the unexpected feelings she provoked within him.

Josh smothered his impulse to blame his conflicted emotions on being in Maryville. He'd never lied to himself before, and he didn't intend to take up the habit at the age of thirty-five. Although snared by a dilemma of his own making, he couldn't escape the fact that Megan Montgomery twisted his emotions into knots.

"Feel better?" he asked when she shifted in his arms a short while later.

"Yes," she whispered against his neck.

"You did your best, Megan, but you can't be the victor all the time."

"I'm not accustomed to failure," she admitted, the keys she still held a reminder of her clumsy handling of a delicate situation.

He peered down at her. Her honesty prompted a kind smile that gentled the harsh lines of his face. "I sensed that about you."

"Do you mind terribly?"

"That you're a tough cookie?" he teased.

She flushed. "No. Do you mind that I'm a bit relentless at times?"

"Only if you go overboard."

"I know now that I can't change your mind, Josh."

"Then we'll agree to disagree."

She nodded as she looked up at him and noticed the intensity of his gaze. Something dark and compelling flared in the depths of his blue eyes. Megan knew in that instant that she should free herself from his embrace, but her common sense faded.

She swayed against him, settling even more contentedly within the circle of his arms and welcoming the bone-softening lethargy brought on by the measured stroking of his capable hands. Megan moaned softly, delighting in the strength and tenderness flowing from his fingers.

"You've got a great body," he said, sounding like a brash teenager who'd just discovered sex.

She grinned even though she knew she shouldn't encourage his blatant sensuality.

"And you've got great hands. You must have been a masseur in another life."

"Hardly," he said in a gravel-rough voice that sent a shattering wave of erotic awareness through her entire body.

His hands continued to drift up and down her back, each stroke enhancing the tension starting to coil deep inside her, each stroke a haunting reminder of the lengthy absence of physical intimacy in her life, and each stroke bringing her into closer contact with the arousal he didn't even try to hide.

Megan leaned back in his arms, her eyes closed and a contented smile on her face.

Josh held her hips with his hands. Fascinated by her dreamy expression, he felt yet another tumultuous rush of desire invade his bloodstream.

"You're a beautiful woman."

When she opened her eyes, Josh glimpsed the sultry promise of her sensual nature. His fingers flexed, digging into her hips, and his body hardened even more.

"Thank you."

"A man could drown in you."

"I'd save him," she whispered.

He smiled then, that same slow, erotic smile that had the power to shake her to her core and level any defense she might devise against his potent masculinity. "You would, wouldn't you?"

She nodded, her clear-eyed expression another indicator of her innate honesty. "Of course. My sister the shrink says I have a classic caretaker personality. It's my destiny."

He gave her a look that made her insides sizzle. "Does that mean you plan to take care of me?"

She laughed. "If the need arises, but would you really ever let anyone care about you that way?"

His gaze narrowed speculatively. "I might be persuaded, but only under the right circumstances."

Reality suddenly shook her. "This is a dangerous game we're playing, Joshua Wyatt."

Tell me about it, he groaned silently, while his body throbbed and his heartbeat thundered in his ears.

"The world is a dangerous place, Megan Montgomery," he said mockingly, and drew her even more snugly against him.

He anchored their hips together with one hand and slid the other one up the length of her spine to her neck. The feel of her warm, fragrant skin, the silken weight of her thick auburn curls, and the lushness of her breasts cushioned against his chest tortured his senses and tested his self-control.

Megan suddenly eased back and looked up at him. No longer able to dismiss her realization that she was playing with fire, she frowned.

Josh forced himself to acknowledge the uncertainty he saw in the depths of her hazel eyes, despite the sensual awareness that linked them like an invisible current of electricity. "You're a temptation I didn't anticipate." As if needing to emphasize his observation, he arched into the softness of her cradling hips.

Unable to stop herself, she reached up and traced his lips with her fingertips. She found his lower lip particularly intriguing. "You have a very sensual mouth."

Josh shuddered. Briefly closing his eyes, he fought for and eventually found the control he needed. As he slowly inhaled and exhaled, he breathed in the lilac scent of the woman in his arms. "I'm hungry for you."

She couldn't dismiss or ignore the arousal that darkened his eyes to a steamy blue and tautened his features. "I'm hungry for you, too," she responded frankly.

"Think of me as a banquet," he suggested in response to her candor and in anticipation of slowly savoring her mouth and then every inviting curve and hollow of her body.

Torn between desire and uncertainty, Megan suddenly tucked her head beneath his chin and held on to him. Josh felt the change in her. Despite his need of her, he knew he wouldn't force the issue.

He held her as they both struggled to bank the desire consuming them. Several quiet moments followed, moments that yielded less frantic heartbeats and steadier breathing.

Josh didn't try to stop Megan when she slipped free of his arms, but he felt a spark of pleasure when she took his hand and laced their fingers together.

"Thank you," she said as they started down the long, circular driveway.

"For what?"

"For not pushing me over the edge when I let

things go too far." She glanced at him. "For being a gentleman."

They paused at his rental car, which he'd left at the end of the driveway. Josh released her hand and dug into his trouser pockets for his car keys. "It seemed appropriate."

"It was, Josh."

"I'm attracted to you. That's not going to change anytime soon."

"I know. I'm drawn to you, too, but we're strangers, and I don't go to bed with strangers, no matter how impulsive my nature."

"Or how turned on you are?"

She nodded, not at all ashamed that she'd responded to him. "You've reminded me that I still have needs and feelings that can't be ignored. It's been a long time since I've cared enough about a man to want to make love with him, but that doesn't mean that I'm ready to dive between the sheets in order to satisfy a momentary urge. I like and respect myself too much to be that shortsighted. I also expect more than a one-night stand when I let myself care about someone."

Amazed by her blunt summation, he clarified, "You do want me, don't you, Megan?"

"Very much."

"What are we going to do about it?"

"Nothing," she said in a voice tinged with regret.

"I didn't plan what just happened."

"I didn't plan it, either, but we can't let it get out of hand."

He leaned back against the side of the car and

crossed his long legs at the ankles. He tugged Megan to his side and slipped an arm around her waist.

"It already is out of hand, but you're right," he agreed. "We need to use our heads."

"Then I guess we should say good night."

He chuckled ruefully, thinking that sleep was the last thing his clamoring senses wanted or needed. Megan glanced at him and met his smile with one of her own.

"I don't expect to get much rest."

"Try," she urged tartly.

"Yes, ma'am."

She reluctantly moved away from him so that he could open the car door. "I really do like you, Josh."

He caught her hand and tugged her back so that she wound up standing between his thighs. "The feeling's mutual."

She studied his shadowed face with the help of the light from the sliver of moon perched high in the sky. "Have you ever let anyone love you, Josh?"

He flinched, but he kept his expression even. "I don't believe in love."

"Then I feel sorry for you."

Josh jerked her forward, the contact immediate, searing, and intimate. "Why don't you feel *me*, instead?"

The cynical nature of his gesture disturbed her, and she mourned the reasons for it, but Megan didn't resist or pull away from him. She didn't fear the aroused state of his body. Neither did his cutting tone of voice produce the anxiety he apparently intended. She simply realized that the incendiary quality of their reaction of each other needed to be dealt with in a calm and thoughtful manner.

"My response to you might be less . . . obvious," she said quietly, "but it's just as painful and equally profound. There's no reason to denigrate what just happened between us."

Her gentleness and candor shamed him. He moved her away from him, turned away from her with a fluid, pantherlike grace, and jerked open the car door.

Megan stayed his actions simply by touching his shoulder. "Don't be embarrassed. I'm not."

He whirled around to face her, his demeanor aggressive and untamed. "Dammit, Megan! Why aren't you like other women?"

"My dad says it's genetically impossible," she quipped in an attempt to defuse his anger. "Montgomery women tend to be on the peculiar side. Apparently, we're not easy to dismiss or ignore."

He swore.

She remained silent. After a moment of consideration, she gently pressed her hand to the side of Josh's face. The stubbled roughness of his beard abraded her fingertips and palm and sent a chorus of sensations streaming into her body. The musky scent of his skin enveloped her as she pondered her unexpected fascination with the wildly unpredictable elements of his personality.

He closed his hand over her wrist, turned his face, and briefly pressed his lips against the warm flesh in the center of her palm.

Megan's knees almost buckled with his sudden tenderness. She impulsively slipped her hand to the back of his neck, slid her fingers through the thick black hair that met his shirt collar, and urged him forward with the lightest pressure of her fingertips.

She hesitated a few inches shy of his mouth and lifted her gaze to the glittering blue velvet of his eyes. "May I kiss you good night?"

He nearly groaned, but he managed not to humiliate himself by begging for exactly what she offered. "If you think you can handle the consequences, Megan."

She smiled and gazed at his mouth.

Josh let her orchestrate their kiss. He accepted what she offered, and neither asked nor demanded anything more.

She held nothing back. She tasted, she tested, and she enticed, but she didn't tease or taunt. She also satisfied mutual need as she indulged her curiosity and desire.

As he felt the trembling of Megan's lips and the stabbing forays of her tongue, Josh clenched his fists at his sides until his fingers ached. Shudders tremored through his large frame. Although he craved the total sensual promise of the woman imprinting herself on his soul, he managed to hold on to his control.

Shaken by the emotional tumult within her, Megan forced herself to release Josh's lips and step back from him. She felt consumed, and she silently cursed herself for giving in to the urge that prompted her to explore the passion of a man who viewed love as fiction.

"Are you all right?" Josh finally asked after several silent moments.

Megan nodded and then steadied herself with a deep breath before attempting to speak. "It's late. I'll see you in the morning." She turned away from him without another word and started up the long driveway.

"Megan?"

She paused but didn't turn around.

Josh ignored the wisdom that cautioned him to let her go. Instead, he approached her, placed his hands on her shoulders, and absorbed the trembling that shook her slender body. "I was right about you. You are like satin-covered dynamite. If it's any consolation, Megan, I can't find a rational explanation for the chemistry between us, either, but it's there, and I don't think it's going to go away."

Still unwilling to face him, she simply nodded and whispered, "Good night, Josh."

Josh stood in the driveway long after Megan closed her front door and extinguished the lights, his thoughts in disarray. The rain soon returned, jarring him from the tug-of-war taking place between his emotions and his common sense. Forced to retreat to his rental car, he reluctantly returned to his temporary lodgings.

Instincts that had served him well over the years encouraged him to leave the matter of Charles Stanton in the hands of his attorneys, but his heart, neglected for much of his life, urged him to remain in Maryville.

Sometime near dawn Josh abandoned his attempt to sleep and decided to stay another day.

Four

At nine the next morning Josh guided his rental car into the driveway of Primrose Preschool. He spotted Megan the instant she stepped out of the house. Clad in a sporty outfit of navy slacks, a thigh-length white knit jacket, and white lace camisole, she glowed with good health and vitality as she made her way down the front steps, a large wicker hamper in one hand.

Megan paused to console a weeping child seated at the bottom of the steps. Josh, unable to surmise the reason for the tears, watched Megan set aside the basket before gathering the little girl into her arms and giving her a reassuring hug.

He could see that the child trusted Megan, because she allowed her to dry her tears, take her hand, and then lead her up the stairs. Megan's obvious compassion for the troubled youngster brought memories of his own childhood to mind.

Although he loathed thinking of his past, Josh couldn't help contrasting Megan's unstinting warmth and affection with the indifference he'd endured as a boy. He recalled his genuine bewilderment at just barely being tolerated by his mother, a woman who considered him little more than a reminder of the betrayal she'd suffered at the hands of her first lover.

Robbed early of his innocence, he grew up guarded and wary. His mother's rejection, he eventually realized, had prompted him to pull into himself, to trust no one, to reject even the most innocent overtures of friendship or concern as he'd hurtled his way through childhood and adolescence with a mammoth chip on his shoulder.

He'd translated his vulnerability and humiliation into a palpable rage against anyone who crossed him. By prowling the streets of Detroit, he honed his survival skills and developed an attitude of disdain for any positive emotion.

He lived and functioned like a wild animal, snarling at the world as he wrestled with the pain of being referred to as "that little bastard" by his mother, a hopeless, bitter junkie who finally overdosed on her son's sixteenth birthday.

Taking her death as a sign that he was free, Josh didn't even pretend to mourn her demise. Instead, he hitchhiked south, his destination uncertain. He wound up being beaten, robbed, and left for dead by a gang of bikers who dumped him behind a roadside diner on the outskirts of St. Louis. The county sheriff who found him took him to a local hospital, paid for his medical care, offered him a place to recuperate, and then proceeded to verbally slap him down every time he grew surly and mouthed off.

Although suspicious of any authority figure, Josh found a secure home with the widower. He slowly let down his guard and discovered a mentor in Sheriff Daniel Cheney. The older man's friendship helped him find a sense of self-worth and spawned a genuine desire within Josh to carve out a place for himself in the world that he could point to with pride.

Armed with a business degree, which was funded primarily by scholarships that Cheney helped him apply for, and his private fantasy that he would one day be able to afford to explore each and every continent on the planet, Josh opened Wyatt Travel. A few years later he mourned the sudden loss of his only ally due to a heart attack, and then invested the life-insurance proceeds in the expansion of his travel agency.

A lone wolf who avoided emotional entanglements, Josh devoted himself to Cheney-Wyatt International, newly named in honor of his mentor. He developed a reputation as a shrewd businessman. Thanks to his workaholic tendencies and his hunger for success, he transformed his chain of agencies into the best in the national and international travel industry before he celebrated his thirtieth birthday.

Josh exhaled quietly, the rush of memories slowing to a stop when Megan pulled open the car door, tucked her wicker basket behind the passenger seat, and then slipped with fluid grace into the empty front seat.

"You look a million miles away," she observed as she fastened her safety belt.

He nodded absently. "I guess I was." Putting the car into gear, he asked, "What's on the agenda this morning?"

"I thought we'd start with an introduction to Maryville, followed by lunch, and then a meeting with Tyler Dunwoody."

"Stanton's lawyer," Josh confirmed.

"That's right. He's in court this morning, so we'll meet him after our picnic."

Josh concealed his surprise and unexpected pleasure as he guided the car through the streets. Everything he saw—from the exclusive neighborhood with its grand mansions, extensive lawns, colorful flower gardens, and trimmed hedges to the equally well-maintained middle class homes that preceded their arrival in the commercial section of town—reinforced his mixed emotions and his resentment that he'd spent his childhood in the poverty and hopelessness of Detroit tenements.

He braked at a Stop sign, looked expectantly at Megan for directions, and caught her staring at him.

"Left or right, Megan?"

"Left," she said hurriedly. Embarrassed, she jerked her gaze to the road. It had been impossible not to be absorbed by Josh's rugged profile, not to run her eyes over his cranberry-colored sweater and black linen trousers. "I wanted you to see the mill. It's Maryville's largest employer."

Josh's frown deepened as they drove through the business district. "I get the impression the old man liked seeing his name plastered all over town."

Megan knew exactly what he meant. "His family—*your* family—founded this town shortly after the Civil War, so it's not surprising that a park, a baseball field, a building or two, or even a street might be named after the Stanton family."

Josh suddenly felt crowded by a past he didn't understand, and he didn't like the feeling at all. "Then why not call the place Stantonville?"

"Mary Halloran, the daughter of a Mobile lawyer who lost his wealth during the war, was the first Stanton bride to be brought here following the war. Her husband, a Yankee carpetbagger from New Hampshire, named the town after her. They were your great-great-grandparents." She risked a look in his direction and saw his startled expression. "It must be strange being given a history lesson about a town that by all rights should have been your home from the time of your birth."

Josh tightened his grip on the steering wheel. "I was watching you earlier with the little girl on the front steps," he commented, changing the subject after several tense moments of silence. "Why was she crying?"

"Her mother's just had a baby, and she feels displaced by all the attention the little one is getting."

"What did you tell her?"

"That it's all right to feel a little jealous, but that she should try to love her little brother as much as she can."

"Sounds like personal experience talking."

She laughed. "I threatened to sell my baby sister when my parents brought her home from the hospital. It took me a while, but I got over my jealousy."

He smiled, easily able to imagine her childish outrage. "You must've been a hellion."

"So I've been told."

Josh pulled into the crowded parking lot adjacent to Stanton Textile Mills. In the process of opening his car door, he hesitated and then glanced back over his shoulder at Megan when she placed her hand on his arm. Easing back in his seat, he faced her and waited for her to speak.

"I've thought a lot about what happened between us last night, Josh."

He scanned her face, noting the slight flush in her cheeks and the uncertainty in eyes. Her skin made him think of fresh magnolia blossoms, and her eyes reflected the gentleness of her heart.

Josh closed his hands into fists in order to keep from reaching out and gathering her into his arms. He sensed that he could lose himself in Megan, but he wasn't willing to risk the emotions required to admit his need.

"And did you come to any earth-shattering conclusions?" he asked.

She nodded, not in the least put off by his

sarcastic tone. She'd already concluded that Josh Wyatt was a man who believed in guarding his emotions. "If we'd met under different circumstances, I'd want to pursue what happened between us. I'm attracted to you, and I think that making love with you would be a wonderful experience."

Her candor rocked him. He felt his body temperature start to climb, but he smothered his reaction to her and remained motionless. "But?"

"As far as I'm concerned, one-night stands are right up there with hit-and-run accidents. I'd feel used if we went to bed together and then parted company."

He smiled lazily at her. "Use me to your heart's content, Megan Montgomery. I wouldn't mind at all."

She refused to be put off by his blatantly sexual comment or by the sensual tension emanating from him, even if the combined impact sizzled her nerve endings. "It simply isn't a good idea."

Heat and desire clamored for attention inside him, but he simply shrugged off his intense reaction to Megan as though indifferent to the entire notion of intimacy. "Then why did you bring it up?" he demanded.

She bristled at his tone. "I *thought* I was being honest with you."

"You're not being honest, Megan," he countered harshly. "You're trying to talk yourself out of something you want. You're also confusing the issue. We'd have sex if we went to bed together. Hot, intense, explosive sex. Nothing more. Lovemaking is a euphemism, and love is a myth."

Dismayed, she took his hand, unfolded his clenched fingers, and stroked his palm with a feathery touch. "You're dealing with a lot of mixed emotions right now, Josh, and you're striking out at me because I'm a convenient target. Intellectually, I understand what you're doing. Emotionally, it hurts when you're sarcastic or intentionally cruel."

He jerked free of her, unwilling to be cajoled or manipulated by her compassion. "Let's get this over with."

Unable to conceal her disappointment, Megan exhaled softly as Josh exited the car and slammed the door. The angry sound echoed in her head as she climbed out and led him to the workers' entrance.

He paused at the door and impaled her with a fury-filled look. "No more armchair psychobabble, Megan. That garbage may work with your preschoolers, but it doesn't cut any ice with me."

She nodded, feeling the blood drain from her face. Turning away from him, she tugged open the door and stepped inside the building.

Regret streaked through Josh. He nearly reached out to stop her so he could apologize, but that would have required an admission on his part that she'd succeeded in penetrating his facade of studied disinterest.

After introducing Josh to the plant foreman, who provided them with safety glasses and ear protectors, Megan commented, "This area is part of the design test center. It's also adjacent to the executive offices. Instead of simply producing undyed bolts of cotton for shipment around the country, Charles diversified the mill." She paused and motioned Josh forward to a wall of glass that provided an encompassing view of the extensive facility, which was a beehive of automated machinery and human activity.

"Charles believed that too many of the Southern mills were failing because of a one-dimensional approach to the business, so he invested in state-of-the-art equipment and persuaded a group of fabric designers and dye specialists to join the operation."

"Makes good business sense," Josh conceded, curious in spite of himself about a man who had apparently possessed the vision to anticipate the needs of both the marketplace and his community.

"In exchange, he gave them creative freedom and an experimental lab that's produced award-winning natural-and-synthetic fiber combinations. Stanton fabrics are competitively priced and in demand around the world. The company even has standing orders from some European fashion design houses."

"What about the workers on the production lines?" Josh asked.

"Excellent employee benefits. Scholarships for their children. Everyone has the option of cross-training, and after five years on the job they qualify for stock options. This is a family operation, Josh, and the employees are loyal. The attrition rate is almost nonexistent. In fact, there hasn't been a layoff of workers in more than fifteen years."

"Impressive."

"And unusual in this age of corporate restructuring," Megan reminded him.

She spent the next hour guiding Josh through the multifaceted test facility. She said little, allowing Josh to observe and question employees at his own pace.

As she watched him, she sensed his surprise at the humanitarian instincts of his late grandfather, as well as a growing, albeit grudging, respect for Charles's business acumen. After discarding their safety gear, Megan and Josh departed from the warehouse-sized work area and entered a long hallway.

Josh paused. "Just how old is Stanton Textile Mills?"

"The hundred and twenty-fifth anniversary celebration was last year. Charles planned it, but he didn't live to see it. The original mill site was leveled by a tornado a few years before the turn of the century. Your great-grandfather, Silas Stanton, was with Teddy Roosevelt's Rough Riders in Cuba when it happened."

Somewhat impressed, he said, "You're kidding."

She grinned. "I wouldn't kid about a thing like that. The Stantons were a pretty colorful crowd. Anyway, when Silas returned from Cuba, he rebuilt the mill. Charles was his only child, and he was groomed to take over all the Stanton interests, which he did when Silas passed on shortly before World War Two."

Before Josh could say anything, an attractive man in his mid-thirties approached them as they navigated the winding hallway. Smiling, he extended his hand in greeting. "You must be Josh Wyatt. I'm Paul Travers, vice president of marketing."

After the two men shook hands, Paul turned to Megan with a concerned expression. "How did Carrie seem to you this morning?"

"She was a little teary-eyed, but she'll adjust to the baby fairly soon."

"That's a relief. Kathy and I have been worried about her."

"Try some time alone with her this weekend at the petting zoo. A little reassurance goes a long way when there's a new baby in the house."

Josh assumed that the Stanton Textile Mills executive and the little girl he'd seen earlier with Megan were father and daughter.

Turning back to Josh, Paul Travers said, "Everyone's anxious to meet you. If there are any aspects of the operation you'd like to discuss, don't hesitate to ask. The entire staff will accommodate you in any way we can."

Josh nodded, taken aback simultaneously by Paul Travers's warm welcome and the fact that the man had his arm around Megan. "I appreciate your courtesy," he said, his tone cool, his narrowed gaze fastened on the male hand absently stroking Megan's shoulder.

"You couldn't have a better tour guide than our Megan. She knows this place as well as the employees." Paul grinned at the object of his praise, gave her an affectionate squeeze, and then continued down the hallway. "She's also a pretty wonderful sister-in-law," he called back over his shoulder, his amusement over Josh's obvious jealousy apparent.

"Sister-in-law?" Josh suddenly felt foolish about the possessiveness and jealousy still stirring inside him, and he couldn't recall ever knowing a woman capable of arousing either emotion in him. Until Megan.

"You heard the man. How about a cup of coffee?" she asked as she led the way to one of several employee lounges.

Josh silently followed her, the lilac scent he now connected solely with Megan filling his senses as they both paused in the doorway of the crowded room.

Megan immediately picked up on the atmosphere of charged expectation. Hesitating, she cast a worried glance at Josh, but he appeared unconcerned about the crowd.

She suggested, "Why don't you stake out a table while I get our coffee?"

Despite the fact that she joined Josh less than two minutes later, she had to work her way through the dozen or so chattering workers gathered around him in order to hand him his coffee. She slipped into the chair opposite him. Although he remained quiet, Megan noticed that he paid close attention to the barrage of comments directed at him.

"Maryville's a good town. You won't be ashamed to call it home," a young man in overalls and a baseball cap assured him. "We'll be starting up the employee baseball teams in another month or so. Come on down to the park and join us, if you'd like."

"You're a mighty welcome sight, Mr. Josh," chimed in another man who appeared to be well past retirement age. Megan knew he was a janitor, one of several employees allowed to work beyond the conventional retirement age. "Old Charlie Stanton died a sad and lonely man. It nearly broke our hearts to see him without kin to call his own."

Megan experienced a moment of anxiety when an older woman clad in a prim shirtwaist plunked herself down in the chair beside Josh's. Megan didn't try to stop the conversation that unfolded, but she listened carefully because she knew Miss Sarah Winston had a blunt manner and a tart tongue.

"You're a handsome devil, aren't you, young man?"

Josh smiled at her, a combination of surprise and pleasure shining in his blue eyes. "If you say so, ma'am."

"And you've got your grandpa's charm to boot," she noted with an approving nod. When Josh's pleasant expression faltered, Miss Sarah placed her hand on his arm and leaned forward. "It doesn't matter a lick to anyone in this town what side of the blanket you were born on. Maryville is your home now, Joshua Wyatt, and we're glad to have you. You're the spitting image of your grandpa, so we all knew right away who you were. My, but that man cut quite a fine figure during his courting days," she reminisced. "I was just a child then, mind you, but every young lady in Maryville was on pins and needles until he selected his bride."

"He doesn't care about that nonsense, Miss Sarah," protested a man clad in a crisp seersucker suit and bow tie.

"Why, of course he does," she huffed. "It's part of his heritage. Besides, who knew Charles Stanton better than his personal secretary? I worked for him for forty-five years. As they say in the world of big business, I know where all the bodies are buried."

A few people tittered. Others looked appalled. Josh laughed out loud. Megan simply smiled, not in the least surprised by the older woman.

Despite her blunt personality, Josh discovered that he did care what Miss Sarah Winston—and the rest of the people in the employee lounge— had to say, although it amazed him that they felt so free to speak their minds to a total stranger. As a businessman, he wouldn't have been surprised if they'd showed resistance, even resentment, toward him.

Josh lifted Miss Sarah's hand and dropped a light kiss on the back of it. The older woman blushed and scuttled back to her cronies on the other side of the coffee room.

"You get read to go fishing, you call Jimmy Wainright, Mr. Josh," added another worker, a middle-aged man with a sun-weathered face and walrus-style mustache. "I'll fix you up with the best live bait hereabouts. And if you've got any questions about your grandpa and his family, you come see me. I'll give you a history lesson. I suspect you need one. Your grandpa was a good man, but his pride hurt him sometimes. He cared about you, even if you didn't know it."

Several others shook hands with Josh and welcomed him with simplicity and warmth. He received invitations to every church in town, several fraternal organizations, and to their homes if he happened to be "in the neighborhood."

Taken aback by their generous spirit, Josh felt emotionally blindsided. He studied the black depths of his coffee, his mood pensive.

Megan reached out and took his hand, worry and uncertainty filling her as a tense silence stretched tautly between them.

Josh finally looked at her. "You set me up, didn't you?"

Five

She heard no anger in his voice, or anything approaching censure, just weary resignation and a hint of bewilderment. Megan's heart ached for him. "I wouldn't set you up, Josh. That wouldn't be fair."

"Then I guess what they say about small towns is true," he concluded. "It really is like living in a fishbowl, isn't it?"

She reluctantly nodded. "Probably even more so where Charles was concerned."

He withdrew his hand from Megan's grasp, pushed his coffee cup away, and flattened his hands on the table in front of him. "I feel like I'm being sucked into quicksand."

"You're not," she insisted in a quietly fierce tone. "You're simply experiencing the collective relief of a community that you've finally come home. Charles didn't have any secrets,

Josh. Unlike most men of his generation, he didn't try to conceal his failings."

When he didn't respond, Megan continued speaking. "The people here know that this is a confusing time for you. Try to remember that when Charles's will was filed, all the documents became a matter of public record. Your identity as his grandson and his only heir also became a matter of public record. He spoke often of his pride in your accomplishments with many of his friends in the final years of his life. Right or wrong, this community is transferring the loyalty and affection they had for Charles Stanton to you. They're sincere and very kind people. Now maybe you'll understand why I love this place so much."

Josh suddenly surged to his feet. His quick movement sent his chair scraping across the tile floor and drew startled looks from several people in the crowded lounge. "Excuse me."

Megan remained seated. She decided to give Josh a few minutes alone. Although she'd intended to introduce him to several of the executives who ran Stanton Textile Mills, she decided that she'd save those introductions for another time. With a heavy sigh she drained the last of her coffee and got up from the table.

Jimmy Wainright ambled toward her as she rinsed out the coffee mugs and put them in the drainer to dry. "How's my Amanda doing at your school for tots, Miss Megan?"

She grinned. "Your grandchild is the most talented finger painter in the bunch."

The older man shifted his gaze to a spot

behind her shoulder. "We wasn't too subtle with that boy, but I'll bet my last dollar that he's got old Charlie's grit."

She smiled. "Let's hope so, Jimmy, let's hope so."

Fifteen minutes later Megan found Josh standing beside his rental car. She immediately noticed the rigid set of his broad shoulders and his stiff-legged stance. Operating solely on instinct, she slipped up behind him, put her arms around his waist, pressed her cheek to his back, and hugged him.

Although he flinched when she first touched him, Josh didn't pull away from Megan. Instead, he covered her hands with his own, bowed his head, closed his eyes, and pondered the unreal quality of the previous twenty-four hours. With confusion dominating his emotions, he couldn't help feeling as though he'd lost control of his world since leaving St. Louis the previous morning.

He'd spent much of his adult life denying his need for the satisfaction of belonging to something enduring, something greater than himself. Not even the international success of Cheney-Wyatt International, had satisfied his deep-seated craving for what he feared was a family.

Torn between the world he'd created for himself and the untested terrain of the world now being offered to him, Josh felt reluctant to embrace the risks involved in the latter. He silently cursed Charles Stanton, Megan Montgomery, and the people of Maryville for feeding a need he'd grown to think of as his greatest weakness and most frustrating vulnerability.

He turned within the circle of Megan's arms and peered down at her. His anger and the pain of thirty-five years of rejection slowly receded as he studied her.

He noticed that her enormous eyes, which held a surprising wealth of worry, dominated her face. Frowning, he lifted his hand and trailed his fingertips down her cheek, his senses registering the satin smoothness of her flawless complexion and the mink thickness of her dark eyelashes.

When he slid his fingers down to the hollow of her throat, he felt the inviting warmth of her skin and the steady throbbing of her pulse. Lowering his head, he hesitated within a few inches of her bow-shaped mouth.

Megan stopped breathing. When she could finally speak, she whispered, "You're looking for motives again, aren't you?"

He absently nodded as he threaded the fingers of both hands into the dense hair that framed her face and tumbled past her shoulders like an auburn halo. "Your hair feels like silk, and you always smell like wild lilacs."

His gentle touch and the confusion and hunger in his eyes made the world tilt to an odd angle. She experienced an inner burst of pleasure that Josh found her attractive. Megan also felt compelled to try to banish his uncertainty. But her personal experience with grief cautioned her that private demons were best vanquished alone.

Josh moved even closer, aligning their bodies so that not even a whisper separated feminine curves from hard muscle.

Crowded suddenly by her awareness of his potent masculinity and the leashed strength of his powerful body, not to mention the burgeoning desire within herself, she clutched his waist. Air surged in and out of her lungs at a rapid pace. "Josh?"

"Don't say anything, Megan."

Wide-eyed, she stared at his mouth. She already knew what he tasted like, and she craved more of the same. Desire streaked through her like a bolt of hot summer lightning, weakening her knees and derailing her convictions.

Megan felt her common sense make a valiant effort to assert itself before she abandoned all caution. "We're behind schedule," she whispered.

"I don't believe in schedules when I'm on vacation," he replied. Still clasping her head with his two hands, Josh tilted her face upward.

Megan felt his breath wash across her skin when he exhaled. Her eyes closed, and she trembled.

When he gently nipped her plump lower lip, their moans mingled. It was the most erotic blending of sounds she'd ever heard.

So much for common sense and schedules, she thought fleetingly as she succumbed to the heady feelings provoked by Josh's tender exploration of her mouth.

The mill's noon whistle shattered the silence of their small world with all the subtlety of an exploding bomb. Josh flinched and released her lips, but he held her in place as he surveyed the area around them.

He watched a seemingly endless tide of workers pour out of the textile mill as he quelled the arousal Megan inspired. Once again Josh realized that no one at the mill seemed threatened by his arrival.

Perplexed and unwilling to believe that they were motivated by simple kindness, as Megan insisted, he couldn't suppress the cynicism that made him wonder if their collective intent was to manipulate him for their own gain.

Was Megan manipulating him, or did she really feel the sensual pull her responsiveness implied? Puzzled and wary, Josh studied her flushed features and speculated on her motives.

"Perhaps we should go ahead and have our picnic," she managed to say in a voice still riddled with desire and embarrassment. "Otherwise, we'll be late for our appointment with Tyler."

Josh pulled away from her, his abrupt movement in sharp contrast to the leopardlike grace she associated with him. He turned, yanked open the door to the passenger side of the car for her, and then walked around to the driver's side.

As he started the car, he belatedly remarked, "Everyone has motives, Megan. The challenge is discovering whether or not they're mutually beneficial. And while I may be up to my armpits in quicksand, don't ever forget that I'm a survivor. Nothing and no one traps me, unless, of course, I'm willing to be trapped."

Josh maneuvered his car around the workers walking to their vehicles in the crowded parking lot. Megan nervously fidgeted with the shoulder strap of her purse.

As they drove back into town, she grew progressively more uncomfortable with Josh's silence. "I didn't set you up. Subterfuge isn't my forte. The people in the test facility recognized you, that's all."

He chuckled, the sound filled with derisive irony. "I'd like to believe you, Megan, but you lack a certain credibility."

Confused, she studied his harsh profile.

He felt her gaze and responded by making a sweeping gesture with his right hand. "There isn't a shred of evidence that anyone in Maryville has been placed in jeopardy by my actions, Megan."

She shifted uncomfortably at the renewed bitterness in his voice. "Not on the surface, perhaps, but there's a lot you don't know about yet because you haven't spoken with Tyler. Look, Josh, I've already admitted to you that I stretched the truth, so don't expect me to apologize again for finding the right button and pushing it."

"That's not the way to win friends or influence people."

Incredulous, she asked, "You aren't even willing to give me the benefit of the doubt, are you?"

"Not where Charles Stanton is concerned."

Megan shivered when she heard the steel in his voice, but she revived her flagging courage, reminded herself to be patient, and addressed his skepticism.

"You've probably already figured this out, but perhaps it bears saying in very clear terms. Charles Stanton was the patriarch of Maryville, just as his father and his grandfather were before him. The townspeople have always looked to the Stanton family for direction and leadership. The people here loved Charles, not only because he was a good businessman, but because he treated the entire community like his family."

Although sensitive to Josh's conflicted emotions, Megan forged ahead, abandoning tact in favor of the unvarnished truth. "You know, I don't think you resent the fact that I stretched the truth, but I am starting to believe that it's totally impossible for you to accept that people are capable of positive emotions like loyalty, compassion, or even love. Has your life really been that empty, Josh?"

Grim-faced, he pulled into a parking space in downtown Maryville. After turning off the engine and removing the key from the ignition, Josh slowly turned and looked at Megan.

She caught a glimpse of the hurt and disillusionment in his eyes. In the next second she watched him conceal his vulnerability and anger behind a shield of arctic blue.

Suddenly aware of their location, she pointed out, "Our appointment with Tyler isn't for another forty-five minutes."

"I want to see him now," Josh said.

"What if he's out?"

"I'll wait."

Megan reached out to him, but he looked at her with an expression of such distaste that she let her hand fall back into her lap.

He exited the car without another word.

She watched him stride across the sidewalk and into the brick building that housed the offices of Maryville's three attorneys without a backward glance. Thoroughly convinced that Josh would never give himself or his heritage a chance, Megan slowly resurrected her composure and followed him into the lawyer's office.

"Tyler Dunwoody?"

A rotund man studying the contents of the open file on his desk glanced up and greeted Josh with a pleasant expression. "You're early, Mr. Wyatt, but you're a welcome sight. Have a seat, why don't you."

After the two men shook hands, Josh sank back into the comfort of a leather wing chair positioned in front of Tyler Dunwoody's massive oak desk. The attorney cleared away the remnants of his fast-food lunch, and then rifled through a stack of files before finding the one he wanted.

Tyler Dunwoody smiled. "It must be pretty disconcerting to discover that everyone seems to know your identity before you even have a chance to introduce yourself."

"That's a fair conclusion," Josh conceded.

He knew the instant Megan slipped into the room, but he didn't bother to acknowledge her presence. Instead, he focused on the lawyer, a sixtyish fellow clad in an expensive but rumpled suit.

The room resembled the man, with its haphazard stacks of file folders, an enormous ficus plant that drooped from lack of water, and a trash can overflowing with discarded papers. Despite the lawyer's appearance and the disorder surrounding him, Josh noted that Tyler Dunwoody possessed the eyes of a hawk.

Megan murmured a subdued greeting and sank into a chair near the doorway. Even though Josh ignored her, Tyler did not.

"You're early, too, Megan, but you're a sight for sore eyes. Make yourself comfortable." He glanced at Josh. "We've got a mountain of documents to go through this afternoon. In fact, we may be at this for a couple of days. Old Charlie's holdings were quite extensive."

"That won't be necessary."

Tyler gave him a questioning look before glancing at Megan. Josh imagined her shrugging dejectedly. The lawyer leaned back in his leather chair, laced his fingers together over his belly, adopted a placid expression, and waited for Josh to explain.

"I won't be accepting the Stanton estate, Mr. Dunwoody. I'd appreciate it if you'd initiate the paperwork necessary to renounce it."

Tyler Dunwoody pondered Josh's comments before remarking, "You do realize that there's no other blood relation and that Charlie intended you as his sole beneficiary."

"That doesn't matter."

The lawyer chuckled. Megan made a soft sound of surprise, but she managed to restrain any further indication of her distress with

Josh's decision when Tyler cast a warning look in her direction.

"I'm afraid it does matter. As much as I love the state of Alabama, I'd hate to see a gang of bureaucrats descend on Maryville, liquidate the assets a family spent three generations building, and then haul millions of dollars back to the capital for deposit in the state's coffers, which is basically what'll happen if you go through with this."

"That's not my problem. I believe I've made my wishes clear, Mr. Dunwoody."

"Call me Tyler. I'll be blunt, Josh, especially given your reputation in business circles. Your wishes are quite reckless." Before Josh could reply, Tyler continued. "There are, of course, several other options available to you, with varying degrees of involvement in the estate on your part. Would you be inclined to consider those options?"

Megan looked hopefully at Josh. After focusing on the human issues of his inheritance, she felt relieved that Tyler seemed inclined to address the potential economic consequences of Josh's actions.

"There are no other options of interest to me, but feel free to itemize them when you present me with the documents required to formally renounce Charles Stanton's entire estate," Josh said flatly. "My mind is made up."

"You've earned your reputation, I see."

"More times than I care to count, I've been called a bastard for reasons other than the unmarried status of my mother at the time of my birth. Frankly, insults are too much like compliments. They simply become tedious after a while." Josh contemplated the attorney through steepled fingers and a narrowed gaze. "If you know nothing else about me, Mr. Dunwoody, know that I rarely change my mind when I make a decision."

Tyler shook his head. "Talking to you is like talking to Charlie Stanton. You're more like him than you realize. He meant well, too, even when he made mistakes."

Disbelief flooding her, Megan exhaled softly. She closed her eyes, rubbed her temples, and silently despaired over the deteriorating conversation taking place between Josh and his grandfather's attorney.

"All right, Josh. All this paperwork's going to take some time, but I'll get started right away."

Tyler Dunwoody reached into his desk drawer and withdrew a cigar. He deliberately took his time snipping off the tip with a small device that he'd tugged from his vest pocket. After lighting the cigar, he puffed enthusiastically until a cloud of smoke began to form over his head.

Annoyed with the lawyer's delaying tactics, Josh cautioned, "I don't intend to leave Maryville until this situation is completely resolved, but that doesn't mean I'm willing to allow it to drag on indefinitely."

Seemingly unruffled, Tyler Dunwoody nodded. "Sounds reasonable to me."

Josh got to his feet. "If you need to reach me, leave a message at the Inn."

Six

The sunny afternoon, the gentle sounds of nature, and the gurgling stream that meandered through the stretch of undeveloped acreage on the outskirts of Maryville soothed Josh in ways that words never could.

He felt the relief and confidence of a man who had regained control of his world. Despite the adversarial nature of his meeting with Tyler Dunwoody, Josh knew that the attorney had no choice but to honor his instructions. Oddly, he liked Tyler Dunwoody, although he didn't feel compelled to cooperate with the man.

Josh stood near the edge of the narrow stream, gazing out across land unencumbered by man, masonry, or machinery. Other than the weathered picnic table situated a half-dozen yards to his right, nothing marred the perfection of the environment. A city dweller his entire life, Josh discovered within himself a profound appreciation for the natural beauty surrounding him.

As he idly pondered the events of the morning, he found his thoughts repeatedly drifting to Megan. He smiled as he recalled her shocked reaction to his suggestion that they go ahead with the picnic she'd planned. A witness to her indecision as they faced each other on the sidewalk in front of the lawyer's office, he understood and even sympathized with her mixed emotions.

He felt no such confusion, he realized as he turned and studied her. He wanted her. He'd desired her, since his first tantalizing glimpse of her sprawled on the Primrose Preschool playroom floor, but he knew now that he craved more than her body and the passion he'd already sampled.

He hungered for this multifaceted woman, a woman who fiercely fought for what she believed in, who redefined words like compassion, sensitivity, and loyalty, and who aroused within him the fragile hope of being cared about for himself and not for what he possessed.

Sighing, Josh wandered back to the picnic table. He felt the darting caress of Megan's gaze, and he saw the bewilderment still lingering in her eyes.

He paused at her side. "Does your family own this land?" he asked.

She shook her head and looked away.

"Is it a secret?"

"I'm just one of several people who watches over the property," she answered.

He voiced a sudden suspicion. "It's Stanton land, isn't it?"

She nodded before making a sweeping gesture that encompassed the terrain all around them. "This is just a small part of what you're sacrificing," she said sadly. "It's more of your heritage, Josh. We've taken care of it for you, just as we've taken care of all the other Stanton assets since Charles died. I hoped . . ."

"You hoped what?"

"I hoped that you'd use the past as a learning tool for the future, not blame an entire community for a mistake someone made thirty-five years ago and then neglected to try to undo until it was too late."

He exhaled heavily, torn between his own feelings and the distress visible in her eyes. He understood her perspective, but he didn't intend to give her false hope.

"Megan, I don't blame the people of Maryville for what's happened. I just wish I'd never heard Charles Stanton's name. I could've gone my entire life without all this aggravation."

Frustrated, Megan buried her face in her hands. "I'm sorry. I know you're tired of hearing all this, but it seems as though my job as the executor for the estate spills over into every conversation we have."

Josh tugged her hands away from her face. He wanted to draw her into his arms and hold her. Instead, he simply presented her with a handful of wild daisies that he'd collected during his stroll. Startled, she accepted his offering and clutched them with both hands.

"You're strangling your flowers."

She flinched and loosened her death grip.

"You'd like to strangle me, wouldn't you?" he asked with a surprisingly compassionate smile.

"The idea had a certain merit when we were at Tyler's office," she conceded, "but I don't feel that way now."

"Shall we start over, Megan?"

Although taken aback by his question, she admitted, "I'd like it if we could."

"I know you're disappointed by my decision, but I'm not willing to explain it or alter it."

Megan's smile faltered. In her role as executor she felt like a complete failure. From a personal perspective she also knew she was poised to relinquish her heart to a man who seemed uninterested in commitment, a hard-edged but vulnerable man who had impossibly high walls around his emotions. In short, Joshua Wyatt personified the exact opposite of everything she'd ever thought she wanted in the man she would love.

Despite all that, Megan consciously set aside every cautionary instinct she possessed. "I've never tried to force the people I care about to adopt my beliefs as a condition for a relationship, Josh. That's not my style. All I want or expect is openmindedness."

"Then you agree that whatever happens between us will remain separate from the final settlement of Charles Stanton's estate?"

"My brain says that's the only thing we can do."

"Good." He grinned, some of the concern he

felt that she would reject him because he had rejected his inheritance receding to a safe distance. "What does your heart say, Megan?"

"That you're dangerous," she quipped as she turned and deposited the somewhat crushed bouquet in a plastic tumbler already filled with water. "Lunch is ready."

Josh sat down at the picnic table and surveyed the buffet of sandwiches, freshly baked cookies, sliced fresh fruit, and two glasses filled with lemonade. "Dangerous?" he finally echoed after several quiet moments.

She gave him a wry look. Laughter danced in her eyes. "My mental health suffers when I'm around you. I never know if I'm coming or going."

"I want to know you, Megan."

Surprised by his intense tone, she said, "But you do."

He shook his head. "Last night you summarized your twenty-plus years of living in less than a dozen sentences."

"Twenty-nine years," she clarified as she handed him a plate and plastic utensils.

"I don't know nearly enough about you."

In search of something, Megan frowned as she rummaged through the hamper. Josh stayed her busy hands, which had begun to remind him of fluttering sparrows, and tugged her down beside him.

"Quit fussing and try to relax. My carnivorous instincts are under control for the moment."

She laughed and folded her hands in her lap. "What exactly do you want to know?"

"What makes you cry?" he asked suddenly.

She answered without hesitation. "Listening to 'The Star-Spangled Banner' before a baseball game, weddings, and failed love affairs."

He smiled. "What makes you laugh?"

"Circus clowns, clumsy puppies, and fireworks on the Fourth of July."

"Patriotic little soul, aren't you?"

She grinned. "And certifiably sentimental, but I'm a Southerner. It goes with the territory."

"What's your proudest accomplishment?"

"Primrose Preschool."

"Who are your favorite people?"

"My family." She paused, gave further thought to her reply, and smiled as she said, "And anyone under the age of five."

Josh chuckled briefly, then his expression suddenly grew very intent. "What makes you . . . want a man?"

Startled, she opened her mouth and promptly closed it.

He idly stroked the tops of her hands with his fingertips. "What makes you want a man, Megan?"

"I'm not sure," she hedged, even though she knew the exact formula. Distill and bottle the essence of Joshua Wyatt and indulge in liberal doses on an hourly basis.

"Make a guess," he urged in a voice resonant with sensuality.

Caution replaced her candor. "I've been in love only once, and what I felt grew out of friendship and compatibility rather than intense passion."

"Sounds pretty tame," Josh observed.

"It was . . . safe," she admitted for lack of a better word. She didn't admit that the feelings blossoming inside her now made all past emotion seem pale, even insignificant. Warmth suffused her cheeks. "I've always hoped there'd be more . . . well, you know, more sizzle if it ever happens to me again."

"You want the fairy tale."

She nodded slowly. "Of course."

"If it even exists."

She heard his skepticism and felt a wave of sadness wash over her. "It exists, Josh. My parents have it, and so do my sisters."

"Define it for me."

She did just that. "Love, passion, laughter, friendship, shared goals, mutual respect, a home, babies . . ."

"I see that you've given the subject some serious thought," he observed with no small amount of amazement.

"Have you ever known a woman who didn't?" she asked.

"I guess not," he admitted. "I've always run like hell when I've seen that particular look in a woman's eyes."

She glanced away before she spoke, fearful that he would notice the yearning in her eyes. "Then you haven't ever been in love."

"You sound very certain of that."

"I am. People rarely walk away from love unless they fear the commitment involved."

Her insight made him uncomfortable and put a defensive edge in his voice. "It's better to end a relationship than to hurt someone by encouraging them to have unrealistic expectations about the future."

She shrugged. "Perhaps." Certain she'd just been cautioned against caring too much about him, Megan reached for the sandwich platter and peeled back the plastic wrap covering it. "Ham and cheese on rye, tuna on whole wheat, or PB and J on white?"

"PB and J?" he repeated.

"You definitely don't hang out with the school-yard crowd. Peanut butter and jelly. I just automatically make them I'm afraid," she confessed. "Sometimes I even add banana slices."

He laughed. "I have to admit that that particular concoction isn't a staple in my diet. I'll stick to the ham-and-cheese and tuna sandwiches."

"No breakfast again?" she asked as she filled her own plate with a sandwich, slices of fruit, and some chips.

"No time."

"The Inn serves a wonderful buffet breakfast."

He arched a brow as he bit into his sandwich.

"My cousin owns the place, and she loves to cook."

He gave her a thoughtful look as he chewed and then swallowed. "Your family reunions must be crowded."

"Like a zoo on a sunny Saturday afternoon. Even I don't know everyone, and I've got the job of updating the reunion roster every year." She wrinkled her nose in concentration. "At last count I think we had about four hundred people on the list."

Amazed at the number, and a little envious,

Josh grew quiet as they enjoyed their picnic lunch.

Megan concentrated on her meal and silently mourned the fact that beyond idle curiosity Josh seemed to place little value on having a family. Although she knew about his background, she still didn't understand why he resisted, and even seemed to resent, both the acceptance of an entire community and their willingness to act as his substitute family now that his grandfather was gone.

Once they finished eating, Megan strolled to the edge of the stream and scattered bits of bread for the birds while Josh loaded the wicker hamper. He joined her when he finished the task, snagged her hand, and asked, "How about a hike?"

"Good idea. I need the exercise after all that food."

He chuckled at the chagrin he heard in her voice. "You definitely have a healthy appetite. Most women pick at their food."

"I never seem to gain weight. My sisters hate that about me. Their secret dream is to see me get as big as a barn when I finally have children. I keep telling them that I have a great metabolism, but they're convinced that I diet constantly."

Josh paused and tugged her up against his body, the thought of Megan swollen with child shockingly seductive. "I wouldn't change a thing about this particular package of dynamite."

"Thank you, kind sir."

"I'm not being kind, just factual."

She smiled up at him and lost herself in the unexpected warmth of his blue eyes. Loving him would be as easy as breathing, she realized.

"Maybe we should go back to town and save our hike for another time?" she whispered, rocked by her last thought.

"Maybe," Josh agreed as he traced her full lower lip with the tip of his finger.

Megan trembled, the impact of his tender touch reverberating throughout her body. Wide-eyed, she stared at him.

Josh lowered his head and touched the seam of her joined lips with the tip of his tongue. He tasted pink lemonade and the promise of passion, and he wanted more.

She moved closer and traced the width of his lips with the tip of her tongue. She tasted chocolate-chip cookies and growing passion, and she wanted more.

They took turns tempting each other until they both shook from the tension of restraint.

Josh changed the rules as he breached the barrier of her lips and teeth and plunged his tongue into the wet warmth of her mouth. He gloried in the sound of the groan wedged in Megan's throat.

When he ran his hands the length of her spine, circled her waist, and then slowly brought his palms upward to cup her breasts, he felt her tightening nipples beneath her lace camisole and flimsy bra. Josh heard her whimper under his mouth as he molded and shaped her with his hands. Touching her, he realized, was like fondling molten flame.

She responded to his intimate stroking by gripping his head with her hands and angling her mouth so that they both found greater access. Moaning, she experienced both relief and escalating desire when Josh grasped her hips and brought her into intimate contact with his loins. She arched against his hardness with tiny bucking motions, desire making her brazen.

Josh dug his fingers into her hips as he absorbed her sensuality. He felt as though he were being hurled into an inferno capable of incinerating his awareness of everything but the woman in his arms.

He abruptly, and very reluctantly, ended their passionate foray when he gentled his embrace, stilled her hips with one hand, and pressed her cheek to his shoulder with his other hand. All he heard for several moments was the harsh sound of their breathing.

When he could speak, Josh said, "I want to make love to you, Megan, but this isn't the time or the place."

Shaken by what had happened, Megan nodded and tried to hide the tears stinging her eyes. She burned for him, and her entire body ached to the point of pain.

"Talk to me," he urged when he felt the faint tremors moving through her. "Talk to me, Megan."

When she didn't respond, he eased her backward and nudged her chin up with his fingertips. "You hurt, don't you, love?"

With tears welling in her eyes, she nodded.

"So do I," he admitted ruefully.

"I'm sorry, Josh. I'm really not a tease."

"There's no need to apologize for something we started together."

She rested her forehead against his chin, took several steadying breaths, and forced herself to calm down. "I don't know what's gotten into me. I'm not usually like this."

He shushed her and cradled the side of her face with the palm of his hand. Josh remained quiet as he considered the explosive nature of the chemistry that repeatedly flared to life between them. He'd never known a woman like Megan, but now he also knew that the protective emotions and nearly disabling desire he felt for her would haunt him long after his departure from Maryville.

In desperate need of distance Megan started to ease free of Josh's embrace. She felt him flinch as she withdrew. Glancing up, she noticed the ruddy color staining his high cheekbones and the tension in his jaw as he gazed out over the rolling green hills.

Instinct more than conscious thought prompted him to snag her wrists and hold her still. "Let's take that walk," he suggested. "We both need fresh air."

"All right." She shifted her attention to the path that edged the stream.

"Megan?"

"Yes?" she answered, not meeting his gaze.

"I wouldn't have been able to protect you if we'd finished what we started a few minutes ago. For obvious reasons, I have some pretty strong feelings on that particular subject."

"You did the right thing, Josh. We shouldn't have gotten so carried away."

"When we make love, I want everything to be right between us."

She nodded her agreement.

After peering at her with a somewhat perplexed expression for several silent moments, he freed her hands. She then led the way down a narrow, tree-lined path that paralleled the stream. As she navigated the uneven trail, Megan sensed that she would be a fool to deny that they would, in fact, become lovers.

She felt an odd mingling of joy and melancholy at the thought of becoming intimate with Josh. Joy because she would be free to physically express her feelings for him; melancholy because she knew he would never become a permanent part of her life.

After nearly two hours of sharing a mutual appreciation for the sumptuous natural beauty of the surrounding terrain, Megan and Josh returned to the picnic area to retrieve the wicker hamper. Josh hoisted it onto his shoulder, and they held hands as they retraced their steps to his rental car. He stowed the hamper in the trunk and then pulled open the car door for Megan.

"I've really enjoyed the afternoon," he told her

as they stood facing each other. "I don't get much time to really relax anymore. My life's turned into a nonstop schedule of business conferences and airport layovers."

"Is this your first vacation in a while?"

He nodded. "Five years."

"Seems a shame. I would think you'd want to take advantage of all the free trips."

"Oh, I do, but always with an eye to the needs of my clients."

"Then take someone along with you who'll force you to relax and have some fun."

He smiled at her. "Are you applying for the job?"

"I'm afraid my personal baggage would include three dozen or so preschoolers. You'd end up using work as an escape route."

Megan hesitated for a moment, her mood growing unexpectedly serious as she recalled a promise she'd made earlier that day.

His smile widened to a grin, and he tapped the end of her nose to get her attention. "Earth to Megan. Come in, please."

Startled, she laughed, the soft sound like a whimsical melody as she looked up at him. With the breeze dancing through her auburn curls, she looked like a green-eyed sprite.

"I'm starting to recognize that worried look of yours. Can I help?"

"Actually, you can," she admitted. "Would you like to go to a party Friday evening?"

"What's the occasion? TGIF, birthday, anniversary, farewell? Give me a clue."

"A welcome-home party."

Josh looked reluctant. "It isn't likely that I know the person, and I'm not a fan of gate-crashers."

She averted her gaze and said quietly, "You're the person."

"Say that again," he ordered, not certain that he'd heard her correctly.

"It's a welcome-home reception for you at the country club. One of my sisters is on the welcome committee, and she mentioned it this morning when she called."

"Welcome committee?"

She heard his amazement. "It was formed last year shortly after Charles died. In anticipation, I guess you could say, of your arrival."

Megan saw him frown and hurriedly said, "The party'll be kind of a flop if the guest of honor doesn't show up. And just think how disappointed everyone will be if they don't get to meet you before you go back to St. Louis."

"And you got the assignment to get me there?" he asked more brusquely than he intended.

She shook her head. "I volunteered."

"Volunteered?"

She nodded, and she knew she couldn't blame the color stealing into her cheeks on the breeze, because it wasn't nearly windy enough to cause a windburn.

"How?"

She understood his question. *How did this happen?* When, she suddenly wondered, did they start speaking to each other in shorthand?

"How, Megan" he asked again.

"That's easy to figure out, if you just think

about it for a moment. My cousin owns the Inn. As soon as you checked in, she put the word out to all her friends, who in turn called all their friends. The rest, as they say, is history."

Horrified by the swift-moving information network that apparently existed in Maryville, Josh sank back against the side of the car. He took his time evaluating the wisdom of attending the social function.

"I'm not staying here. St. Louis is my home," he reminded her.

"That's all right, Josh. They still want to meet you."

"I don't like misleading people."

"You won't be. Tell the truth if someone brings up the subject of the estate. Otherwise, don't mention your decision if you don't want to have to explain yourself."

"Then why even bother to go?"

"Think of it as a thank-you gesture," she suggested. "You could've easily encountered suspicion and resistance in Maryville. Instead, you're the reluctant recipient of the hospitality of an entire community. Not your average situation, is it?"

"Hardly," he agreed quietly as he grappled with his amazement.

"Josh, people simply want to meet you and wish you well. If you take the entire situation at face value, then it won't become complicated or uncomfortable."

"Will Tyler Dunwoody be there?"

"Probably, but he's not about to advertise the fact that he's failed to persuade Charles Stanton's heir to accept his inheritance. He'll have to deal with that soon enough. Tyler isn't a man who likes to seem foolish or inept, despite his rather slipshod appearance."

His gaze narrowed. "You'll have to deal with the fallout, too, won't you?"

She winked playfully at him. "I'm tougher than I look. I'll survive. In the meantime, why don't we just have some fun? You're the one on vacation, right?"

"What time shall I pick you up?" he asked, aware that his desire to spend more time with Megan, as well as his curiosity about the townspeople's real feelings concerning his status as Stanton's only heir, formed the foundation of his decision to attend the party.

Megan grinned and threw her arms around him.

Josh held her tightly against the lean, hard strength of his body. Once again desire leapt to life within him, leaving in its wake a raft of tiny brushfires that lingered even after he released Megan and assisted her into the car.

As they drove back into town, he teased, "If I'd had an inkling of your enthusiasm level at the outset of this conversation, I wouldn't have made my decision so quickly."

She laughed. "You just like to torture me. And you can pick me up at six."

"Care to fill me in on the dress code?"

"I'm wearing a cocktail dress."

"Something red and slinky, no doubt."

Megan smiled thoughtfully as she recalled the black lace dress hanging in her closet, the very outfit she intended to wear to the country-club party. "How else would I be able to drive you utterly witless with desire?"

"You've already managed to do that, Megan."

"Oh, goodie," she crowed. "I'm having the best time practicing my feminine wiles on you."

"They're very effective," he assured her. "Too effective."

Her laughter, along with her smile, faded, and in a serious tone of voice, she admitted, "I feel happy when I'm with you, Josh."

He glanced at her, his eyes a smoldering shade of blue reminiscent of the passion they'd recently shared. "That's a two-way street, Megan Montgomery."

Josh returned his gaze to the late-afternoon traffic as he drove through the center of the prosperous Alabama town. He felt his own hunger for the acceptance of the community expand with every hour he spent in Maryville and with Megan, and it worried him.

"What's the agenda for this party?" he asked in an attempt to redirect his thoughts.

"Cocktails, dinner, and dancing," she answered.

He whistled in astonishment. "These people move fast, don't they?"

"They want you to feel welcome, and it doesn't take long to put this kind of thing together."

Josh paused at a red light and looked at her. Nothing, he realized, in his lone-wolf existence had prepared him for the sense of vulnerability he now experienced. "I feel overwhelmed, Megan. Just overwhelmed."

She reached over and covered his hand with her own. "You've got at least one ally that I know of."

Although he concentrated on the ebb and flow of traffic, Josh didn't release Megan's hand until they arrived at her home. He said little, but he appreciated both her reassurance and her compassion.

Seven

Early that Friday evening Josh and Megan paused at the coatroom just inside the country club. Slipping out of her wrap, Megan exchanged the garment for a ticket stub provided by the woman behind the counter.

She tucked the ticket into her evening bag and turned to Josh. Megan experienced a moment of pure delight when she saw the appreciative look on his face.

"I hope this town has a qualified cardiac-care unit."

"Planning a heart attack?" she asked with a grin.

"Of course not, but I feel great empathy for anyone in the general vicinity with a faulty ticker." Josh tugged Megan into a quiet alcove when several laughing and chatting people walked into the foyer of the country club. "You should've warned me about your dress, Megan."

"This old thing?" she teased.

"I would've hired a contingent of security guards."

"You don't approve?" she inquired, knowing full well from the gleam in his thick-lashed blue eyes and the possessive feel of his hands on her shoulders that he did.

Josh released a muffled groan. "Of course I approve, but so will the rest of the male population of Maryville. I have visions of spending the next few hours beating them all off with a large stick."

"It's just a simple black lace dress."

"Maybe on a flat-chested nine-year-old. That material's hugging you like an old friend." He briefly reinspected all the territory below her sparkling hazel eyes, broad smile, and gloriously curly auburn mane. "Don't get me wrong. It's an incredible dress, especially on you, but I'm amazed that you can even breathe in that little number."

"Stretch lace gives."

"Trust me, Megan, on you it doesn't just give, it molds, teases, tempts, and then seduces."

She pressed her fingertips to the side of his face before reaching up and smoothing back a lock of jet-black hair that had fallen across his forehead. "Are you tempted?"

Josh captured her hand and pressed a hot kiss directly into the center of her palm. "I've been tempted since the moment I walked into Primrose Preschool."

"So have I," she whispered, suddenly overwhelmed by the depth of her feelings for him.

Megan's admission prompted him to ask, "Can we leave now?"

She laughed and hugged him. "I'm glad you like my dress, but I think we should hang around for a while. At least through supper."

Taking her hand, Josh tucked it into the crook of his arm, squared his shoulders, and guided her down the hallway to the banquet room. Along the way he murmured suggestively about all the ways in which he planned to repay her for sending his heart rate into overdrive.

"Sounds interesting," she commented with a straight face the instant before she introduced Josh to her high school English teacher.

Along with the mayor, members of the city council, and executives from the Stanton Textile Mills, among them her brother-in-law Paul Travers, Megan stood beside Josh in the receiving line. She lost count of the number of introductions she made.

As the evening unfolded, she couldn't decide whom she felt proudest of—Josh, who epitomized the polish and style he'd acquired at the helm of Cheney-Wyatt International, or the cross-section of Maryville residents, who greeted their guest of honor with genuine warmth and hospitality.

While she noticed that Josh still seemed amazed by the friendliness of the townspeople, Megan refrained from assuring him of their sincerity. She sensed that he needed time to assimilate everything that had occurred since his arrival, as well as time to reflect on and measure the depth of the welcome being offered by the community that was his heritage.

Despite Josh's stated intention to remain in Maryville only as long as it took to assemble and sign all the documents required to renounce the Stanton estate, Megan still hoped and prayed that he would change his mind. If he didn't, her personal loss would be as profound as the loss to the community as a whole.

After a splendid meal, Megan indulged in some much-needed fresh air on the terrace. She concluded that pushing Josh to change his mind at this juncture, or attempting to exert even the subtlest influence over him, would be a mistake. She'd done far too much of that already.

Because she finally grasped the depth of his conflicting emotions, Megan understood that Josh needed time to make a decision he could live with. No one, she reasoned, possessed the right to disrupt the stability and professional success he'd found in St. Louis, or to interfere in his life. She silently vowed to respect his feelings, no matter what the emotional cost to herself.

The sound of footsteps on the brick terrace distracted Megan from her thoughts. Turning, she saw Josh strolling toward her. He carried two partially filled brandy snifters.

"Still feeling overwhelmed?" she asked as she accepted the after-dinner drink.

He smiled as he leaned back against the black wrought-iron railing. Slipping an arm around

Megan's shoulders, he drew her against his side before answering her question.

"I guess I must be adjusting." He paused briefly for a sip of brandy. "No one's asked me any controversial questions, and Tyler's treating me like a bad case of the flu. All in all, I have to admit that the evening is progressing more smoothly than I originally expected."

"Tyler's not a fool, Josh."

"I agree. He's also as clever as the proverbial fox. I'll have to keep an eye on him." Idle speculation regarding the lawyer's motives gave way to warm appreciation as Josh studied Megan with the aid of the moonlight. "How about you? Are you enjoying yourself?"

She smiled up at him. "I'm having a wonderful time."

"You seem . . . subdued. Are you tired?"

She shook her head and smiled gently. She heard the band start its first set of the evening with a familiar ballad—a particularly haunting melody about an ill-fated love affair.

Megan glanced away, very nearly crippled by the surge of unexpected emotion that filled her. After she'd spent so much of the evening fantasizing about being in Josh's arms, the music seemed to emphasize the futility of wanting someone who seemed disinclined to linger in her world.

"Want to have an ever better time?" he asked.

She looked up at him, as tremors of despair and desire rippled through her. Unable to speak, Megan simply nodded in reply.

Josh relieved her of her brandy snifter and

placed both their drinks on a nearby table. He then drew her into his arms, transforming Megan's fantasy into reality.

She surrendered to the intimacy of the moment, and savored the inherent strength and leashed power in Josh. Molded breast to chest, pelvis to loin, and thigh to thigh, they formed a single entity as they moved in seductive harmony.

"Is that you, Megan?"

She heard Josh's low groan and soft curse just before he pressed a kiss to her forehead and loosened his embrace. Megan slowly lifted her head. She felt mildly disoriented, as though she'd just awakened from a lengthy sleep.

"I'm sorry to interrupt," said the intruder, a slender woman with short strawberry-blond hair. In her late thirties, she bore a striking resemblance to Megan. "But I need to talk to you for a moment."

Looking at Josh, Megan promised, "I'll meet you inside in a few minutes."

Although he nodded his understanding, she saw the regret in his eyes that their privacy had been disturbed. After retrieving his brandy snifter, Josh strode across the terrace and into the banquet room. Megan took those much-needed moments to collect herself before she faced her sister.

"Problem, Kathy?"

"I had no idea that you two were so involved. He hasn't been in Maryville all that long, has he?"

"We're just friends."

"Try again."

"You said you needed to talk to me," Megan patiently reminded her.

Kathy Travers gave her a concerned look. "It's been ages since you've even been out with a man, Megan. Josh seems very nice, but do you know him well enough to—"

"He is nice, Kathy."

"That's it? He's nice? The postman's nice, Megan. So's the butcher, but they're both pushing sixty and have grandchildren."

Megan remained silent.

Concern was etched in Kathy's features. She moved closer and placed her hand on Megan's shoulder. "Why so closemouthed?"

She shrugged negligently. "I guess I don't have anything to say."

Kathy frowned. "Are you certain you're all right?"

"Of course."

"Megan Montgomery, you couldn't lie to save your own hide as a kid, and that obviously hasn't changed in all these years."

Tears welled in her eyes, and she felt grateful for the muted terrace lighting. "Kathy, I know you mean well, but please don't prod me about Josh."

Relentless, but also obviously sympathetic to the telltale emotion in Megan's voice, Kathy asked, "You're falling in love with him, aren't you?"

Unwilling to confirm or deny her sister's speculation, Megan nonetheless understood Kathy's ingrained need to protect as well as to periodically orchestrate the lives of her younger siblings, but she lacked the energy to go several rounds with her at the moment.

Kathy admitted, "I was going to ask you to keep the baby tomorrow so that Paul and I could spend the day with Carrie, but I think I'll ask Mom instead."

"Maybe you should."

"Now I know something's wrong. You always fight tooth and nail to watch the little ones in the family."

Determined to maintain her privacy, Megan caught her sister's hand and briefly squeezed her fingers. "Ask Mom this time, but remember to ask me the next time." She drew in a steadying breath and managed to add brightly, "Now why don't we go inside? Paul probably thinks you've gone home without him."

Megan spotted Josh the instant she stepped into the room. Clad in a severely tailored pinstripe suit, he stood head and shoulders above several members of the local city council, who appeared to be hanging on his every word.

Relieved when he glanced in her direction, she watched him smile ruefully and then shrug as if to say, "Unless you rescue me, I'm trapped for the duration."

She began working her way through the clumps of chatting people who blocked her path to Josh. Forced to pause several times when friends tried to draw her into their conversations, which centered primarily on Josh Wyatt's arrival in Maryville, Megan finally made it to his side.

Smiling at the people clustered around him, she boldly announced, "Ladies and gentlemen, I'm officially kidnapping our guest of honor. Rumor has it that he's a wonderful dancer."

Josh guided her to the dance floor. "Have I ever told you that directness is one of your finest qualities?"

She grinned as he pulled her into his arms. "I guess that means you like pushy women?"

"This feels very familiar," he commented as they fitted their bodies together and moved to the music. "And for the record, Ms. Montgomery, I happen to adore every pushy bone in your body."

"I'm so glad, Mr. Wyatt," Megan whispered, responding to his playful leer. "I certainly wouldn't want to be guilty of disappointing you."

He peered down at her, his eyes suddenly blazing hot desire. "You couldn't ever disappoint me, Megan."

Oblivious to her surroundings, she kept her gaze locked to his. Sensitive to every aspect of Josh's body, Megan absorbed the heat emanating from him and welcomed the growing proof of his desire.

They danced until the hour grew late. Only a few other couples lingered in the banquet room and on the dance floor, among them Kathy and Paul Travers.

Locked in a tight embrace, Megan and Josh continued to sway to an invisible melody even after the band completed the last waltz of the evening.

Megan was breathless and almost painfully aroused. A soft sound escaped her, a wholly spontaneous acknowledgment of the tension spiraling wildly out of control deep in her abdomen.

She felt a corresponding burst of tension ripple through Josh. She blinked in surprise when he stopped moving altogether and she discovered that the dance floor and the banquet room were deserted.

Josh tightened his hold on her when she began to ease out of his arms. Lowering his head, he whispered quietly but purposefully, "Your scent has changed, Megan. I'd being consumed by the erotic essence of lilacs and musk. Your essence."

She trembled as the meaning of his words penetrated the sensual haze enveloping her. "Josh?"

"Yes?"

"It's late."

"I know."

"Time to go home?"

"Please."

He slid his arm around her waist. After retrieving Megan's evening bag, they departed the banquet room.

"Did you see those two, Paul?"

Megan's footsteps faltered at the sound of her sister's voice.

"What's . . ." Josh began, but she raised a hand in warning and shook her head.

"Which two?" In the process of helping his wife into her coat, Paul Travers spotted Megan and Josh as they paused in the shadowed hall-way. He nodded when Megan placed her finger to her lips, signaling that Paul should refrain from alerting Kathy to her presence.

"Megan and Josh Wyatt."

"Sure. They were dancing. So were we."

"They were dancing the way we dance at home."

Paul smiled awkwardly at the object of his wife's comments. "So?"

"They were practically making love on the dance floor."

"So?" he said again.

"Don't be dense."

Paul grinned. "Now that I think about it, he *was* pretty possessive about Megan this morn-ing when I ran into them at the test facility."

"You didn't tell me that."

"I didn't think it mattered."

"Of course it matters. What exactly hap-pened?" Kathy demanded as she pawed through her purse. "I can't find the car keys."

"I hugged Megan like I always do. I thought Wyatt was going to deck me until he realized we were related by marriage," he remarked as he reached into his jacket pocket and produced the missing keys.

Unwilling to embarrass her overprotective sis-ter, Megan began to inch backward. Josh stilled her, a look of genuine amusement on his face.

Paul winked at Megan and Josh and then gently nudged Kathy toward the door. "Let's not inter-fere."

"I never interfere," Kathy protested. "I'm just worried about my sister."

Megan stifled the laughter churning inside her.

"Your sister is levelheaded, past the age of consent, single, and she's obviously finished mourning Tom. No matter how good your intentions, she doesn't need you to poke your beautiful nose into her affairs."

Megan silently blessed her brother-in-law for giving her sister such good advice.

Josh muttered, "Bravo!"

She nearly giggled when she heard the sound of two people playfully smooching before the country-club front doors slammed shut.

Laughter shook Josh as he tugged Megan into his arms and hugged her. "She's utterly priceless."

"She's a royal pain, but she means well."

"I always wanted brothers and sisters when I was a kid, but I get the distinct impression they're a mixed blessing at times," Josh remarked as they walked out.

"Truer words were never spoken," she agreed.

Megan savored the contentment she felt in Josh's company as he drove his car through the nearly deserted streets of Maryville. Regret that their evening together would end momentarily sifted into her consciousness the instant he pulled into the driveway and parked the car.

They sat in silence for several moments. With a soft curse Josh gathered Megan into his arms and kissed her with incredible tenderness.

She sensed a change in him, but she couldn't fix a label to it or define the reasons for it. Whatever the cause, the harsh defensiveness that he'd worn like armor during their first hours together seemed absent, a banished sentry no longer required to guard his emotions.

"I should go in now," she eventually whispered as she rested her head against his shoulder and stroked the side of his face with her fingertips.

"It's late," he agreed, echoing her earlier sentiment a heartbeat before he turned his head and drew her fingertips, one by one, into his mouth. Silently promising himself that he would leave soon, he sucked the tip of each finger very gently at first, but the inner heat licking steadily at his senses escalated his desire to flashpoint in seconds.

Megan shuddered, the wet warmth and tugging motion of Josh's lips and the raspy feel of his tongue sending desire spinning into her bloodstream like a dervish in a mad whirl. She felt the stark heat of his passion as he trailed the tip of his tongue across her palm and then kissed the inside of her wrist.

Megan's pulse throbbed at a hectic pace against his lips. Josh abandoned restraint in favor of an overwhelming need to absorb her very essence, the essence of wild lilacs and musky heat that threatened to cripple his self-control even as it promised ultimate satisfaction.

She heard his groan as he continued to lick the delicate skin of her inner wrist, and the compelling need thriving within her prompted her to shift her body so that she wound up sprawled across his chest.

Her hair tumbled forward across her forehead and cheeks and spilled over her lace-covered shoulders like a silken cloud as she crouched over him. Josh tunneled his fingers into the auburn mass, clasping her head and holding her still as he found her lips.

Megan sighed unsteadily. Clutching Josh's shoulders, she parted her lips and welcomed his heady kiss. His pliant lips, darting tongue, and nipping teeth drove her to such a point of breathless exhilaration that her senses hummed and her grasp of the world became suspended.

His kiss exceeded her every expectation and assured her that lovemaking held a multitude of possibilities her limited experience had not revealed. She hungered for each and every one of those unknown possibilities, but only with Josh.

He seduced her with his lips. He expressed the urgency of his own desire with sweeping strokes deep in the interior of her mouth and teasing, skimming forays across the even line of her teeth with his tongue. He devoured her like cotton candy and then proceeded to search out and discover other delights of texture and taste.

Josh also explored the curves and hollows of her shapely figure with gentle, searching hands. Megan felt bolts of hot summer lightning zing across her flesh. Her breasts grew swollen with need and her nipples tightened to tense points of sensitivity, while low in her belly a craving that defied rational description expanded until she knew it was on the verge of consuming her.

When Josh unexpectedly shifted his hips, Megan found herself being lifted and then situated intimately between his thighs. She felt the strength and power of his arousal and automatically arched into him, instinctively seeking, mindlessly searching, for the fulfillment of the need blazing within her heart and body.

She cried out when he wrenched his lips from hers, and she collapsed against his chest, her face buried in the hard curve of muscle and sinew where his shoulder and neck met.

When he could speak, his voice sounded frayed. "I need you, Megan."

"I want you," she whispered, her voice strained by intense desire and physical anguish.

Josh managed to untangle their bodies, exit the car, and lift Megan into his arms in a series of fluid movements that seemed almost dreamlike to Megan. Although her fingers shook, she found her house key in the bottom of her evening bag and unlocked the front door.

Josh climbed the stairs to her bedroom with Megan still cradled in his arms. He carefully lowered her to a standing position in front of him, the strain of the desire raging within him evident in the shaking hands that drifted across her shoulders and down her arms.

Aware that his candor might come with a high price, he cautioned, "I can't promise you the fairy tale."

She caught her lower lip between her teeth and nodded, her eyes enormous in her pale face. "I don't want promises that won't be kept, Josh, but I do want you."

Eight

Josh watched Megan slowly turn around until
her back was to him. Fascinated by her graceful
movement, he waited while she lifted her hair
out of the way and revealed the zipper at the
nape of her dress. He was aware of the trust
inherent in her unspoken invitation, and lowering the zipper, he slowly exposed her slender
back. The light from a small lamp on a nearby
table cast a golden glow across her fair skin.
When she lowered her arms, Josh smoothed the
fabric off her shoulders and down to her waist.

Bending to her, he skimmed her hair aside
and pressed his parted lips to her nape while he
released the catch of her bra. He felt Megan
tremble and heard the ragged sigh that escaped
her. With his lips still whispering over the delicate skin at the base of her neck, Josh drew her
even closer by slipping his hands beneath her

arms and then sliding his fingertips along her rib cage.

He paused at her narrow midriff, his fingertips pressing points of fire on her warm, satin-smooth skin. When he cupped the generous weight of her breasts, Josh heard yet another sound pass her lips, a barely audible whimper that sent a shaft of desire straight to his core.

He alternately shaped and molded her breasts before he gave in to temptation and rolled her nipples between his fingertips until they grew rigid with arousal. Breathing in her unique lilac scent, Josh buried his face in the curve of her neck and fought for control as she shuddered repeatedly beneath the erotic torture of his knowing hands.

Pleasure and disbelief filled Megan. Her heart fluttered madly in her chest and her knees came close to buckling as Josh tenderly assaulted her sensitive skin. Desire engulfed her, drowning her senses and making her arch against him.

Josh froze, his already ragged breathing suspended for a long moment as she squirmed against him. He finally exhaled, the sound harsh in the silence of the room. Shaken by the overpowering need burning in his loins and coursing through his bloodstream, he reluctantly released her.

Megan took an uncertain step forward, hesitated, and then turned to Josh. When she lifted her head and looked up at him, her flushed cheeks and rapid respiration revealed that she, too, felt overwhelmed by raw desire.

Slowly, seductively, and with her gaze fixed on

Josh's face, she eased her dress over her hips and allowed it to fall to the floor. Her slip and bra immediately followed.

Clad only in skimpy black panties, garter belt, and hose, Megan stood before him like a pagan princess from the past. Enthralled by the invitation in her eyes, Josh swiftly shed his jacket, tie, and shirt.

They simultaneously reached out to each other, their senses achingly alive, their bodies aflame, and their emotions carried along on a swift current of mutual desire. Swinging her up into his arms, Josh carried Megan to the four-poster canopy bed and carefully placed her on her back.

After discarding what remained of his clothing, he knelt between her parted legs, gently eased her garments from her, and then ever so slowly ran his fingertips from the inside curve of her ankles all the way up to the apex of her thighs. As he left a trail of tiny brushfires in his wake, he knew that he'd never seen anyone more beautiful, more vulnerable, or more deserving of being cherished than Megan.

The thatch of auburn silk at the top of her legs beckoned, but he forced himself to wait. He moved over her, teasing her inner thighs, her belly, and her breasts with hot kisses and fevered hands.

Megan writhed beneath him, her hands clenching and unclenching, her legs moving restlessly, and her hips hungrily straining for more. His features, so taut and strong, reminded her of chiseled stone, and his touch, so powerfully erotic, swept her into a chasm of even greater need.

She cried out and clutched at Josh's head and shoulders when he began to sip from her flesh.

Simultaneously tugging and stroking her nipples with his fingertips, and applying his darting tongue to the mysteries hidden in the dark cleft between her thighs, he savored her musky lilac scent and taste, just as he savored her wet inner fire and halting cries.

Sudden, wrenching pleasure imploded within her. Her body quaked with a force that made her heart race and her senses shatter. She cried out Josh's name when the sensation finally crested.

He gathered her limp body into his arms, holding her as the tremors slowly ebbed and left her in the throes of a shivery aftermath that seemed without a beginning or an end.

With fluid grace and strength Josh shifted both their bodies until he sat on the side of the bed with Megan perched atop his powerful thighs. Claiming her mouth, he again devastated her senses and revealed the manner in which he would soon claim her body.

Under the steady stroking of his hands and the insistent desire conveyed by his consuming kisses, Megan felt her strength and splintered sanity slowly return. She brought her legs up and around Josh's hips, her knees bent and her heels crossed behind him.

He inhaled sharply at the sight of her, and his large hands skimmed down her back and over her hips. With one hand looped around his neck to steady herself, Megan reached for his arousal in the same instant that Josh's fingertips skimmed down her belly and discovered the humid depths of her passion.

Both flushed with desire and, breathing erratically, they watched each other as they simultaneously stroked and teased.

Megan silently marveled over the silken heat and straining power beneath her fingertips. When Josh shuddered under her hands, she saw his features tighten and his eyes darken. She leaned forward then, licking and nipping his throat and shoulders as she continued her exquisite manipulation of his maleness.

A willing victim of Megan's sensual nature, Josh's flesh surged and throbbed within her grasp. Tension coiled like a tightly-wound spring deep in the pit of his belly, and his fingertips, gliding in and out of her heat and stroking her swollen flesh, tremored faintly with the control he exerted over himself.

"Don't make me wait any longer, Josh," Megan finally whispered in a broken voice.

Her plea shattered his control, and his eyes snapped open to see the dazed hunger in her eyes.

Breathless, Megan slumped against him. Josh reached for his discarded trousers and quickly found the object he sought in one of the pockets.

Megan plucked the foil packet from his hands once he opened it, leaned back, and said softly, "I wish we didn't need this."

"I don't want you ever to regret that we were lovers," he said to her in a voice laden with regret that they couldn't be totally free with each other.

Although her heart tripped at the reminder that he would eventually leave her, she gently smoothed the moistened protection into place. She let her fingertips linger in the dense curls at the base of his abdomen, exploring the coarse texture of his body hair before circling even lower to stroke and explore and tantalize.

His body jerked suddenly. "Megan!"

Alarmed that she'd done something wrong, she looked up at him. "I'm sorry. I didn't mean to hurt you."

"The only pain I feel is not being inside you," he rasped harshly as he lifted her, shifted her forward, and then slowly lowered her until she surrounded his aching shaft.

A hissing sound passed her lips, and her fingernails dug into his shoulders as her body stretched to accommodate him. Somehow he found the strength to go slowly with her, but he soon realized that she refused to be swayed by his tactics.

With each provocative up-and-down gliding motion of her body, Megan's consuming heat lured Josh deeper and deeper into the heart of her passion. Her legs gripped his waist, her fingers were embedded in his shoulders, and her head was thrown back in utter abandon.

With burning muscles and straining limbs Josh paced himself against her seductively writhing body. He felt as though he'd been cast into a pool of molten liquid, and he knew in a stark instant of mental clarity that leaving Megan would be his worst nightmare come true.

Emotion swamped him, hurling him into a mindless quest for completion. Streamers of flame converged on his senses, setting them ablaze. He surged upward, again and again.

Megan accelerated her already frantic movements, and when she cried out, Josh felt tremor after tremor ripple through her. Each one traveled a path directly to his heart, consuming him, branding him, devastating him. Absorbing the deep contractions shimmering within her, he felt them flow through her like a series of massive tidal waves. Josh drew exquisite pleasure as he experienced the full force of her release.

Finally, her body went slack, and he held her close. In the throes of the most profound physical and emotional experience of his life, he lost the ability to think or reason. His awareness of anything but his rioting senses and Megan, who had become the center of his world, disappeared. With a cry he willingly yielded to the force overpowering him.

When he finally found the strength, Josh clasped Megan to his heart and sank back across the rumpled white lace comforter, altered forever by what they had just shared.

Neither spoke.

Neither moved.

Their mutual craving for a peaceful aftermath to the explosive firestorm that had just overtaken them kept their bodies joined. When their breathing slowed, they eventually drifted upon a sea of silent harmony.

Megan approached wakefulness slowly after a deep sleep. She exhaled, the sound a soft echo of her contentment as she shifted from her side to her back.

The mild ache that lingered in the lower regions of her body didn't worry her. Neither did the sensitivity of her breasts and nipples. She understood the cause, and she embraced the memory with a smile.

She reached out, thinking to embrace the man responsible for her happiness, but she found only empty space and cool sheets.

Thunder, not surprising given the storms that had been rolling across the Southeast in recent days, crackled and rumbled low across the sky. Megan felt the house shudder.

Bringing herself up to rest on her elbows, she glanced at the clock to confirm the time and then at the French doors on the far side of the room when lightning lanced across the sky. A lingering flash in the predawn darkness revealed Josh sitting in a chair across the room. Megan caught a glimpse of his ruggedly chiseled profile and muscular body.

She drew herself up until she was half-reclining against the pillows plumped against the headboard. Another flash of lightning caught Josh in midstride as he crossed the room. He switched on the lamp on a night table and paused at the side of the bed. Aware that she probably looked like a mess, she ran her fingers through her tousled locks.

"I've never known anyone like you, Megan."

She laughed. "You mean you've never known a woman who needed a hairbrush at the ready twenty-four hours a day?"

His silence prompted Megan to lower her hands and smooth her fingertips across the sheet bunched at her waist. She resisted the urge to cover her exposed breasts.

"I've never know a woman who believes in fairy tales," he admitted with a frown. "And I've never known a woman capable of redefining words like 'erotic' and 'sensual.'"

Her eyes skimmed his body. She didn't look away when she saw his burgeoning arousal. Megan shifted when she felt a rush of heat invade her bloodstream. The pulse points in her body started to throb with primitive desires and emotions.

"Your body is already starting to soften and heat, isn't it, Megan?" Josh lowered himself to the side of the bed and reached out to stroke the delicate pink tips of her breasts. They peaked instantly, inviting another caress. "You're hungry for me again, aren't you?"

Unwilling to deny the obvious, she simply nodded. Megan heard a low groan escape him before he pulled back and studied her with an intentness she'd never seen in his expression before.

"I can't help what you make me think and feel, Josh."

"I didn't plan on someone like you." He thrust

his fingers through his thick black hair. "Dammit, Megan, why did you have to be a part of all this?"

"Fate," she quipped, hoping she could lighten his mood.

He said nothing. He simply peered at her from beneath dark brows shadowing cool blue eyes. She studied him, tracing his strong nose, even stronger chin, hard, beard-shadowed cheeks, and sensual mouth with her gaze as she sat up and moved toward him. She didn't care about her nakedness; she didn't care about anything but banishing the bleak look from Josh's face.

Reaching out, she deliberately trailed her fingertips up and down his thigh, her nails making tracks in the dense dark hair that covered his muscular legs.

His lips thinned to a hard line. "What am I going to do about you, Megan?"

"You're going to come even closer to me," she urged, disturbed by the anguish in his voice. "You aren't going to think about anything outside of this bedroom, and then you're going to relax and let me make love to you."

He covered her stroking fingers, stilling her relentless touch. She responded by placing her other hand on his abdomen, and she immediately felt the clenching of the muscled plane.

She absorbed the shudder that went through him with her fingertips. Pleasure and desire mingled within her as she urged him onto his back, but she paused, her hands suspended above his thighs when he cautioned, "Don't let yourself care too much about me, Megan. It won't work, and you'll wind up getting hurt. That's not something I want to see happen to you."

Unwilling to accept his warning, she clasped him between gentle fingers before stroking up and down the thick length of him. He reminded her of heated silk layered over a stick of the most volatile dynamite.

"Do you understand what I'm telling you?" he demanded, passion and something Megan couldn't quite identify putting an angry edge in his voice.

She leaned over him, her breath washing across his sensitive flesh as she spoke. "Of course I understand, but your warning's too late."

"I can't care back," he protested through gritted teeth when she leaned closer still and touched her tongue to him. He groaned when her lick turned into an openmouthed kiss, but he managed to warn, "That part of me died a long time ago. No one can resurrect it. Not even you."

She hesitated, her heart weeping for the isolation and hurt he'd obviously known. "The ability to care doesn't ever really die, Josh. It just needs to be nurtured. If you'll let me, I'll prove it to you."

She took his silence as permission to show him without words a small portion of what caring and loving could mean. She pressed her lips to him, teasing him with delicate, catlike strokes of her tongue while threading her fingertips through the dense curls clustered around the root of his maleness. Satisfaction filled her when she heard a groan of mingled disbelief and pleasure escape him.

He curved the hand that wasn't gripping a fistful of bedding around the back of her head. When he began to thrust his hips upward, Megan understood and accommodated his craving.

She felt every shudder that shook him, and heard yet another moan spill from him, the sound gloriously stimulating.

As she continued to caress him, and as she absorbed his salty taste and musky scent, she felt the pull of her own heightening desire deep inside. Relief filled her when she felt Josh's fingers slide up her inner thigh and find her heat and the dampness beyond. She moaned, savoring the sensations she caused and the ones she received.

Megan suddenly sensed how easy it would be to love him. And then she realized that she *did* love him—and would forever.

Josh shifted from beneath her hands and mouth, dragged her up his body, and tucked her under him in a swift, fluid movement that left her breathless, smiling, and flat on her back with Josh looming over her.

"You're sneaky," she accused as she lifted her arms and looped them around his neck.

"And you're hell on my self-control," he countered as he fitted his hips between her thighs and pressed his manhood against the sensitive folds of her body.

A delicious shivery sensation rippled through

her entire body. "I've never wanted to do that before," she confessed.

Josh stiffened, and his eyes narrowed. "Why now, and why me?"

She bit her lip, dismayed that Josh considered her feelings for him, and perhaps even her reason for wanting to make love to him, suspect.

"Do you really need to ask?"

His head dropped forward and he muttered a curse, but Megan thought the word sounded oddly gently as it passed his lips. She clasped his face between her palms and forced him to look at her. She hated the caution she saw in his expression.

"Don't worry. I'm not trying to trap you. I just want you to know that what we're sharing is very special to me."

He exhaled sharply, but he didn't try to warn her off again. Instead, he pressed his hands to the sides of her breasts, massaging them so that her nipples brushed his chest hair time and time again.

She trembled, violently this time, and then she whimpered when he abruptly bent down and took one of the hard peaks into his mouth. Sensation flooded her, making her arch upward. Her hips and legs stirred restlessly.

She felt the sturdy power of his loins pressing against her, tempting, teasing, never getting quite close enough, driving her insane with wanting. Determined to have him buried inside her soon, Megan reached for him.

Breathing raggedly, Josh pulled away from

Megan despite her whimper of distress. Seconds later he returned, his mouth seemingly insatiable as he drew sustenance from her lips. Her body caught fire as he plunged into her depths and his tongue surged into her mouth.

They clung tightly to each other, bodies fused, arms and legs tangled, pace frenzied, and restraint abandoned as they sought mutual satisfaction.

Flashes of lightning continued to fill the sky. Thunder rumbled and shook the house, but the storm outside paled when compared to the emotional and physical storm raging between Megan and Josh.

They crested suddenly and simultaneously, their releases claiming them with a wrenching intensity.

Rocked by the sustained force of their climax, they held fast to each other. Sanity returned slowly. Time passed as they listened to the angry storm raging outside. Both still trembled from the aftershocks of their slowly receding passion, but neither one had the strength or the inclination to speak.

Nine

When Josh finally got up and hastily dressed, Megan decided not to alert him to the fact that she was awake. She remained silent, watching him through barely parted lashes as he wandered around the bedroom.

She held her breath when he paused at the side of her bed, and she couldn't help wondering about his thoughts and feelings. She doubted, however, that Josh would share them with her.

Joshua Wyatt was, she reminded herself, a man who didn't believe in love, a man who shunned emotional commitment. She sighed softly when he turned away from her and walked to the door. Only then did she open her eyes.

Megan sensed his eagerness to leave, but he surprised her when he hesitated at the door and glanced back at her. Although unable to read his expression, she nonetheless met his probing gaze without revealing the sadness that had already begun to invade her heart.

"Good morning," she managed to say. "It must be late."

"It is."

"Shall I set your mind at ease, Josh?"

"About what?" he asked, a suspicious edge in his voice and a scowl on his face.

A wave of melancholy mingled with her sadness, but she fought both negative emotions and kept her voice even as she spoke. "What we shared last night and just now was the most beautiful experience of my life, but I haven't forgotten your warning. I don't expect a commitment from you just because we made love. All right?"

He shrugged, seemingly unaffected by her words. "Whatever you say."

Megan slid to the edge of the bed in a tangle of sheets. She freed herself, revealing her nakedness before she slipped into the robe draped across a nearby chair. Turning, she asked, "Do you have time for breakfast?"

"You have a beautiful body, Megan."

As she smoothed her hair back from her face, she smiled and tried to exude a calm she didn't really feel. "Thank you."

"I'm not hungry," he told her in a belated response to her earlier question.

"You're sure you wouldn't like some juice or coffee before you go?"

Stop trying to keep him from leaving, she warned herself. He regrets what happened, and you can't change how he feels.

"No."

"I'll walk downstairs with you then."

"There's no need."

"I'd like to stretch my legs."

"Fine."

He jerked open the door and stepped aside. Megan moved past him, but she stopped abruptly when Josh placed a hand on her shoulder.

"Are you all right?"

Startled by his question, she looked first at his hand and then at his face. In her mind's eye she also suddenly saw their naked bodies joined in passion, and she remembered the feel of his hands on her.

Megan shivered, the image slowly fading as she focused on Josh. The intensity burning in his eyes and her memories made her reach out to him, but he shrank back from her touch.

"No morning-after nerves, and no . . . physical discomfort," she assured him as she struggled to protect emotions that felt flayed by his coldness. "Thank you for asking."

He seized her hand, his grip almost crushing her fingers. "Don't thank me, Megan."

She felt her temper uncoil and then flare to life, and she didn't try to stop the sarcasm that tinged her next remark. "You're a skilled lover, Josh, and you obviously care about my health, so why shouldn't I thank you for being courteous?"

Looking as though she'd just slapped him, Josh dropped her hand. "It makes you sound . . ."

"Callous? Aloof? Devoid of emotion? Uncommitted?" she demanded, implying that he seemed all those things to her at the moment.

"Don't do this, Megan," he ground out through gritted teeth.

"Don't be honest with myself?"

"Don't hurt yourself on my account," he said. "I'm not worth it."

She felt her anger prepare to flee. She longed to wrap her arms around him and tell him that he was worth any sacrifice and all the patience she possessed because she loved him. But she knew he would reject her words and all the emotions they entailed.

Loving anyone, Megan realized, would make him vulnerable. Why shouldn't he protect himself? a small voice in her head asked while defeat rolled through her. Why shouldn't he? she thought sadly.

"You aren't listening to me, Megan. I said I need the keys."

Confused, she frowned. "Keys?"

"To Stanton House."

"Oh!" she exclaimed. A fragile kernel of hope instantly lodged in her heart. "Of course. They're downstairs. I'll get them for you."

A few minutes later Megan dropped the key chain into his open hand.

"This doesn't mean anything significant," he cautioned.

She nodded, trying to understand his motives even though she sensed that questioning them would be futile. She watched him slowly close his fingers around the keys before he lifted his gaze to her face. She didn't find a single clue to his state of mind in his enigmatic expression.

Although deeply concerned for him, she kept her voice even and reminded him, "You'll find the diaries I mentioned the other day in the library. The room is locked, unlike the other rooms in the house, and I'm the only person who's been in there since Charles died. You'll want to use the narrow brass key to open the library door."

He nodded absently as he moved away from her, fists clenched at his sides and his knuckles white with tension.

"If you need anything, Josh, I'll be here all day. Saturday's my only chance to clean and restock the preschool supply room."

He gave her a final probing look before he said, "Good-bye, Megan."

She whispered a faint good-bye as he walked out the door without a backward glance.

Megan sank to the bottom step of the staircase, stunned by the finality in his voice.

Megan attempted to piece together her fragmented emotions with a long soak in the tub, but the inactivity drove her to distraction long before the bubbles floating atop the warm, scented water started to dissolve. After hurriedly washing and dressing in scruffy jeans and on old T-shirt reserved for housecleaning, she dragged a brush through her long tresses and worked it into a loose, chubby braid that extended halfway down her back.

Determined to overcome the frustration caused by Josh's rejection, she launched into a cleaning frenzy intended to obscure him from her thoughts. Within a few hours the preschool glowed, the scent of detergent and glass cleaner replacing the accumulated grime of a week's work of sticky fingers and playtime activities, but Josh Wyatt still hovered in her consciousness.

She broke her vow to ignore his presence at Stanton House when she paused before the front playroom windows. Because his rental car remained parked at the end of her driveway, she felt safe in her assumption that he had chosen to linger and explore his heritage.

Megan hoped that he would find insight and understanding within the pages of Charles Stanton's personal diaries, but she also feared that much of what he discovered would hurt him.

By the time midafternoon rolled around, Megan's nerves felt as taut as newly strung piano wire. She fought the urge to cast caution to the wind and confirm for herself that Josh was indeed all right.

Tyler Dunwoody inadvertently solved her dilemma when he called in the midst of her efforts to restock the preschool supply room. Fifteen minutes later, her face newly scrubbed, a lunch tray balanced in her hands, and bearing a message for Josh from her uncle, Megan arrived at the side entrance to Stanton House.

She found Josh seated in the library, the faint scent of rum-soaked tobacco often enjoyed by his late grandfather lingering around him. Surrounded by files, scrapbooks, and leatherbound journals, Josh's expression was somber and fatigue shadowed his eyes.

"I come bearing a snack and a message from Tyler."

Josh silently cleared a space at the edge of the desk.

Megan smiled hopefully. "How about a PB and J? The kids tell me that it cures everything from a skinned knee to hurt feelings, so I've learned to swear by them."

"I know you mean well, Megan," he said quietly.

She looked up from the lemonade she'd just poured. "I don't know if I mean well. Maybe I'm just being nosy. I can't figure it out at the moment, and I don't expect you to, either. The bottom line's really simple, Josh. I care about you, and I'm worried about you. Trips down memory lane can be unsettling, especially if the memories you're discovering are unexpected."

He waved a hand over the books and papers littering the top of the desk. "You're familiar with all this stuff, aren't you?"

"Most of it," she admitted slowly. "Charles insisted. He thought you might need help coming to grips with everything you'd discover here."

Josh exhaled heavily, massaged his temples, and then ran his fingers through his hair in a gesture that reminded Megan of the frustration she'd experienced in recent hours.

"I don't need my hand held, but thank you for lunch," he said.

Stung by his dismissal, she observed, "I'm not a nurse and I'm not your mother, Josh, so I don't plan to hold your hand. I'm simply offering my friendship."

"And your body," he said very, very softly.

"And my body," she echoed, certain now that he placed little value on what they'd shared. "I'm sorry I bothered you," she went on woodenly. "When you're finished with the tray, just leave it in the kitchen. I'll get it later."

Josh rose from his chair. "Megan, I . . ."

She paused in her flight to the door, but she didn't turn to look at him.

"You have a message for me from Tyler," he reminded her.

Shaken once again by his emotionless tone, she felt her heart jerk to a stop. When it resumed beating, she managed to speak calmly in spite of the pain. "He expects us at his office on Tuesday morning."

"What time?"

She turned and caught a glimpse of his hard features before she answered. "Eleven."

"I'll see you there."

"All right," she whispered.

Forgive me, Josh almost shouted. I don't know what I'm doing or what I'm feeling right now. But he remained tight-lipped and frozen in place.

Mired in self-disgust, Josh watched Megan walk out of the library, her spine stiff and her arms wrapped around her middle as though someone had struck her with a fist. He had delivered the blow, he knew, however figurative it might be.

He came close to going after her, but he sank back down in his chair instead. Grappling with his need for her and his fear of her rejecting that staggering need, he felt incapable of offering or receiving any kind of comfort.

Somehow, Josh vowed silently, he would find a way to apologize to her, because he no longer doubted her sincerity or her compassion. He did, however, doubt his worthiness of her generosity and warmth, despite the bottomless well of hunger deep within him that yearned for a woman like Megan.

For the moment, though, he felt compelled to continue his study of Charles Stanton's diaries. Still reeling from his discovery of his own life history among the old man's personal papers, obviously the result of the efforts of several private investigators, Josh also found himself in the position of being forced to deal with the regret and pain his grandfather had chronicled.

He wanted to believe that Charles Stanton regretted his interference in his son's life, interference that had robbed Stanton of a grandson and Josh of a stable family life. He easily understood the pain the old man had written about, because it reflected the anguish of the childhood he'd endured, an empty childhood that had dogged his footsteps into adulthood, prevented him from sharing his feelings, and kept him from trusting others.

Stunned as well by Stanton's repeated written

statements of his pride in his grandson's evolution as a successful businessman, Josh slowly began to see himself through new eyes. On the fast track for so many years, he rarely dwelled on his professional and financial successes. He simply set goals for himself and single-mindedly set about accomplishing them.

He also learned of his grandfather's conviction that Josh possessed the ability to provide the leadership and guidance necessary for the continued well-being of Maryville. Amazed by his confidence, Josh felt both gratified and overwhelmed by it.

Day faded into night.

Josh remained in the library, slowly paging through scrapbooks that contained his past and the past of the family he'd never known, absently snacking from the tray Megan had delivered.

Touched by Stanton's despair regarding his only child's penchant for fast cars, even faster women, and his fatal attraction to alcohol, Josh saw that the old man blamed himself for ruining his son's life by pampering him and then failing to provide parental guidance in time to avert the tragedy that took his life.

Having spent most of his own life wrestling with feelings of love and hate regarding his mother, Josh also grasped Stanton's apprehension that his son had chosen the wrong woman as a prospective bride. He confronted the complete truth when he read the itemized list of her drug-related brushes with the law, although he was already aware of his mother's checkered past.

The hour grew even later, but Josh ignored

the periodic chiming of the clock above the mantel. When he discovered that Stanton had learned of his grandson's existence four years after his birth only because his mother had attempted to extort a large sum of money, Josh knew that he finally had a more complete picture of the past.

Resentment began to seep out of him. The sense of betrayal he felt at his mother's hands shifted to pity. While her bitter, self-involved nature had robbed him of his rightful identity, she had been an unknowing catalyst in his quest for respectability and success.

As he closed and stacked his grandfather's personal journals, Josh realized that he shared many qualities with Charles Stanton, not the least of which was pride. Stanton's decision to observe Josh's life from afar might have been a mistake, he reasoned, but at least the old man had tried to rectify the situation.

Sometime after midnight, Josh locked the library and left the house, having begun the process of forgiving Charles Stanton for his mishandling of family relationships. As he walked out to his car, he recognized that he'd gained more than an education about his heritage by coming to Maryville.

Armed with a clearer picture of the past and the insight necessary to find peace within himself, thanks in large part to Megan's determination, Josh spent much of the next two days driving aimlessly around the Alabama countryside.

He finally realized that Megan, who was never

far from his thoughts, had been right. He needed to understand and forgive the fallibility of others. He also sensed that if he could find the courage necessary to conquer the demons that haunted him, then he would find the peace he craved.

Just as he had begun to see himself through Stanton's eyes, Josh viewed his inheritance and the close-knit community of Maryville with new eyes. He now believed that the Maryville community and the Stanton assets resembled a sacred trust. Rejecting the estate out of hand vanished as an option, but Josh still required time to consider and evaluate the true extent of all the Stanton holdings.

Introspective by nature, he also promised himself time to determine if he was the right person to seize the Stanton torch and carry it into the future, but first he intended to focus on the feelings Megan aroused in him.

She touched his heart in a thousand different ways, rekindling within him a yearning to be loved. He longed to believe that her feelings for him went beyond the instinctive kindness and compassion of her personality. For the first time in his life Josh felt a willingness to risk revealing emotions that might be rejected by Megan.

Seated near the door, Megan watched Josh stroll into Tyler Dunwoody's office at precisely eleven o'clock on Tuesday morning. Clad in a jade-green pullover, navy corduroy slacks, and leather deck shoes, he appeared rested and relaxed, not at all the aloof and extremely indifferent man she'd last seen in the Stanton library two-and-a-half days earlier.

She felt a sudden anger with his demeanor, but she battled to keep her temper from igniting. She pressed her shaking hands together, aware that her tension of the last few empty days and sleepless nights showed in her pale face and in her rigid body. She silently watched Tyler and Josh greet each other and shake hands.

Tyler gathered the documents stacked in front of him. Glancing at Megan, he frowned. "You don't look well, young lady."

"I must be a little under the weather. It's allergy season, so perhaps it's my turn for a case of the sniffles."

She felt Josh's gaze on her, but she refused to look at him. She needed all her strength to remain in control while he cavalierly discarded his heritage, dismissed the economic welfare of the entire community, and walked out of her life.

"Hello, Megan."

Silently cursing him, she nonetheless responded. "Good morning, Josh."

Preoccupied with the task at hand, Tyler moved from his desk to a long conference table. Josh joined him. Megan slipped out of her chair and silently followed the two men, her hands closed into fists and pressed to her sides.

"Do you have any interest in hearing some of the options I mentioned the last time you were here?" Tyler asked.

"This isn't the right time," Josh began. "What I think we should do is—"

"What you should do is have your head examined," she muttered just before something snapped inside her and she jerked the stack of documents out of Tyler's hands.

"Megan!" the lawyer exclaimed.

"Megan," Josh said softly. "You don't understand."

"Oh yes, I understand. I understand completely."

She slammed the documents onto the conference table. As the two men looked on, she snatched a clump of pages, tore them in half, and dropped them. They scattered all around her feet. She repeated the action several times, her anger and frustration so consuming that she didn't pause.

Breathless and trembling, Megan finally stopped, drew in a lungful of air, and stared at the debris littering the floor. Looking up, she snapped, "Close your mouth, Uncle Tyler, or you'll draw flies."

Josh grinned at her after smothering a chuckle. He wanted to throw his arms around her and hug her until she calmed down. He wanted to tell her that she was the most spontaneous, outrageous, and wonderful woman he'd ever known, but good sense and a healthy respect for Megan's current state of mind prompted him to remain still and watchful.

Megan let the last of the shredded pages fall from her hands. She scowled at Josh, his amused expression sending a flash of fury into her bloodstream. "This isn't funny! You're making me crazy, Josh Wyatt!"

He sobered and calmly asked, "Feel better now?"

"Much!" she cried, although in truth she felt like a deranged idiot. Tears filled her eyes, and her chin trembled.

Josh moved toward her. "Megan, there's no . . ."

The gravity of what she'd just done descended on her like a falling boulder. Horrified by her recklessness, she turned and charged for the door, grabbing her purse on the way out, tears of embarrassment and frustration streaming down her cheeks.

Josh started after her, but Tyler grabbed his arm and stopped him. "Let her go, Josh. She needs a few minutes to settle down. I've got all this stuff on the computer, so I'll just print up a new batch. Why don't we try again this afternoon?"

Not really hearing the lawyer, Josh absently nodded as he pulled free and sidestepped the mess on the floor.

"Josh?"

He turned in the doorway, responding to the urgency in Tyler's voice.

"Don't be angry with her. She was very close to Charlie Stanton, and she knows what's going to happen to the town once you leave. What you're about to do is killing her, so try to understand."

Josh exhaled quietly, then promised, "I'll give you a call, Tyler."

Josh made it outside in time to see Megan swiping at her tears as she drove away. Concerned for her safety, he got into his rental car, and discreetly followed her as she drove back to Primrose Preschool.

Ten

Still reeling from shock at her actions while at Tyler's office, Megan pulled up into the driveway, turned off the ignition, and slumped back in her seat. She breathed slowly in and out, calming herself as best she could before going inside to face the controlled chaos of the preschool.

The sound of a car door slamming registered on the perimeter of her mind. Lifting her head, she glanced in the rearview mirror and spotted Josh. Groaning, she reached for her purse and exited the car. She knew she couldn't delay facing him. As she mentally prepared herself to offer the apology she owed him, she wished she could postpone it until later.

Her footsteps faltered when she heard someone shout, "Get the school van! We don't have time to wait for an ambulance to arrive."

Two teaching aides, one carrying the limp body of a small child, emerged from the hedge-lined path at the side of the house. Megan immediately recognized her niece.

She met the trio in the middle of the driveway. "What happened?"

"She took a header off the top of the slide, Miss Megan."

"When?" she demanded as she gathered Carrie into her arms

"Just a minute ago," the other aide answered.

Megan nodded. "Don't alarm the other children. Find Kathy and Paul. Their phone numbers are listed in Carrie's file. Have them meet me at Stanton Memorial."

Megan didn't resist Josh as he guided her into the front seat of his vehicle. He had them out of the driveway and rolling swiftly down the street in a matter of seconds.

"Three blocks east and then a right?" he asked, revealing his growing knowledge of the Maryville city streets.

"Yes," Megan whispered, her gaze on Carrie's still form and closed eyes.

Josh glanced at Megan. "She'll be all right."

She raised pained eyes and looked at him. "I'll never forgive myself if she isn't."

"Think positive," he urged. "When you expect the worst, it usually happens."

The emergency-room staff, already alerted to their impending arrival, stood ready to receive the little girl. An orderly transferred Carrie from Megan's arms onto a gurney for transport into an examination room. A moment later a clerk shoved a clipboard into Megan's hands, instructing her to complete the attached form.

Megan stared after Carrie. Medical personnel clustered around the child, who still hadn't moved on her own. Megan took a step forward, then another. The clipboard slipped out of her hand and clattered onto the floor. She kept moving forward, her expression dazed.

Josh approached Megan and gently slid his arm around her after bending down to retrieve the clipboard. He guided her to a bank of seats in the empty emergency-room waiting area.

"Megan, listen to me." He took one of her hands and was instantly alarmed by its chillness. Warming it between his two larger hands, he patiently reminded her, "You couldn't have prevented this, so don't blame yourself."

"I'm responsible for the children, Josh."

"But you aren't God."

Startled, she released a shuddery sigh, and with the fingertips of her free hand, slowly rubbed her temple. Finally, she straightened in her chair, her voice gaining strength as she spoke. "I'd better fill out that form."

Josh shook his head. "Just give me the answers. You're too shaky to handle a pencil right now."

They spent the next five minutes working together. Megan looked up when a nurse approached them, her heart in her throat as she waited for the woman to speak.

"Are you the child's parents?"

"I'm her aunt," Megan answered.

"And the parents?" the nurse prompted.

"Kathy and Paul Travers. They're being notified."

"She's a minor."

Megan understood her point, although Josh looked baffled.

"I'm authorized to approve care," Megan assured the woman. "But I believe you already have a presigned permission slip from her parents for complete medical care in the event of an emergency." Her voice cracked as she finished speaking.

The nurse's manner softened. She placed a reassuring hand on Megan's shoulder. "It'll be a while before we know what we're dealing with, so settle in, have some coffee, and I'll keep you advised."

Megan nodded.

Taking his cue from the nurse, Josh questioned, "Coffee?"

"No, not right now." She glanced at him, his gentleness and compassion finally registering in her mind. "Thank you. I don't know what I would've done if you hadn't followed me home."

Once again he drew her into his arms. Megan melted against him, closed her eyes, and found strength in the security and warmth of his embrace. As she listened to the steady beating of his heart, she felt the sting of tears and tried to suppress them, but she failed.

She wept silently, for her fear that her niece might not regain consciousness and for the loss she already felt at the prospect of Josh's departure from Maryville. She considered her life without him, and felt overwhelmed by the utter bleakness of it.

"Megan! Where's Carrie?"

Megan wiped the tears from her face and jumped to her feet to embrace her sister. She quickly explained what she knew of Carrie's mishap and her unconscious condition.

Kathy informed the clerk of her identity before turning back to face her sister. "Carrie dove headfirst at me the other day from the top of the staircase. It's a miracle that I managed to catch her, so please don't think I blame you for this. She's too fearless for her own good."

Grateful for her sister's attitude, Megan rejoined Josh. Her mother and Paul Travers arrived fifteen minutes later. Another one of Megan's sisters, Kelly, hurried into the waiting area while Paul and Kathy spoke briefly with the doctor.

An orderly wheeled the gurney bearing Carrie out of the examination room. Megan felt her heart twist painfully when she caught a glimpse of the little girl, who appeared dwarfed by the adult-sized conveyance and the portable oxygen unit lodged beside her prone body.

Kathy and Paul hovered on either side of their daughter for a few moments before turning to face family members. Both badly shaken, they visibly fought for control.

Megan watched her sister swallow her tears and square her shoulders while Paul spoke. "She hasn't regained consciousness, so the doctor's ordered a series of tests. He suggested that we use the fourth-floor waiting room. It could be a long afternoon."

Quiet until now, Josh commented, "I have an

acquaintance in St. Louis. A neurosurgeon. Shall I ask him to fly down?"

Startled by Josh's offer, Paul struggled to compose himself. "Thank you, Josh, but the staff here is top-notch. Carrie's in good hands. Your grandfather made certain of it when he built the hospital and recruited the medical personnel."

Josh realized that Paul's reference to Charles Stanton didn't bother him. In fact, he felt a certain pride in his grandfather's farsighted-ness. He simply nodded his understanding as he put his arm around Megan's waist. "My offer stands if you change your mind and want a second opinion."

"I appreciate that." He glanced at his wife, who smiled tearfully at Josh. "We both do."

Megan remained at Josh's side while Paul led Kathy and the others down the hallway to the elevator.

Once they were alone, Megan looked up at Josh. "That was very generous of you."

"Your sister and her husband should have the best for their daughter. I'd want the same for my own child."

She smiled and willingly went into his arms when he tugged her forward. She suddenly longed to give him the gift of fatherhood, but she doubted she would ever have the chance. After long moments of holding each other, they made their way to the fourth floor.

The afternoon passed slowly, the sun inching across the sky, then descending to the horizon.

Restless and on edge, Megan noticed that

everyone took a turn pacing the hallway outside the waiting room. She nearly collapsed with relief when the head of the hospital's neurology department finally visited them and voiced cautious optimism that Carrie would soon regain consciousness.

Although food was the last thing on her mind, Megan urged her mother and Kelly to help her get coffee and sandwiches from the cafeteria. She suspected that neither Kathy nor Paul would want to leave the waiting room, but she hoped that the availability of food would encourage them to eat.

Megan's father, a third sister, and one of her brothers arrived in time to share the meal in the waiting room. Although curious about Josh's presence, they simply introduced themselves and joined the vigil.

Worried that he might be intruding on the Montgomery family, and feeling somewhat overwhelmed by this close-up view of genuine family unity, Josh debated the wisdom of a discreet exit, but Megan's grip on his hand and the flash of alarm in her eyes when he asked if he should bow out convinced him to remain.

Seated beside her a few hours later, with his arm around her shoulders and her head cushioned by his broad chest as she dozed, Josh recalled her comment, "We're always there for one another."

He believed her now, despite his previous skepticism. As he listened to the soft sound of her relaxed breathing, he contrasted the stark emptiness of his own childhood with Megan's family.

He discovered that his hunger for love and support seemed to be growing in intensity. Perhaps, he reasoned in his characteristically analytical manner, because he could see the vitality and warmth in Megan's family relationship firsthand.

Josh felt Megan shift in his arms. When she sat up and stretched, he decided that she needed a reprieve from the interminable wait. "How about a walk to get rid of the kinks?" he asked quietly.

She nodded. "I'd like that." Megan paused briefly at her mother's side to explain her departure.

Josh noticed the approving smile Megan's mother flashed in his direction. Oddly pleased by her response, he smiled in return. Hand in hand, he and Megan descended to the hospital's rose garden.

Primarily used by patients and visitors, the deserted garden reminded Megan of an island of serenity. They strolled the flagstone paths in companionable silence, surrounded by the warm, humid night air and the scent of hundreds of rose blossoms.

Megan paused at the foot of a small waterfall, the centerpiece of the garden. Appreciative of Josh's quiet strength, she turned to face him. "You've been incredible today. After the way I acted this morning . . ." She fell silent when he pressed his fingertips to her lips.

"I care about you and your family, Megan."

"That's why I'm grateful."

"I don't want your gratitude, and you should know me well enough by now to realize that I do only the things that I really want to do."

She laughed, surprising herself and Josh given the singularly humorless quality of the day. "My favorite mule."

He tried to scowl at her, but a smile tugged at the edges of his mouth. "I suppose I should thank you for not calling me a jackass."

"There's an interesting thought," she teased.

"Your family's quite remarkable."

She sobered, recalling his earlier hesitation to be drawn into her family circle. "We're like most families, Josh. We love, we fight, we help one another, and we interfere in each other's lives. Pretty typical family stuff, from what I can tell."

"Typical only if that's what you're accustomed to," he observed.

She studied the hard lines of his face in the subdued lighting provided by the fixtures at the base of the waterfall. "Have you ever considered having a family of your own?"

"Not really."

"Why?" she whispered, sadness suddenly overtaking her.

He shrugged and looked away. "No time. No one to share it with. No"—he cleared his throat—"no frame of reference on which to base the concept."

"You didn't know anything about the travel industry when you graduated from college, but you created Cheney-Wyatt through hard work and determination," she reminded him. "You turned a dream into a reality in an incredibly competitive industry. Why not do the same thing on a personal level?"

"I don't know if that's possible for someone like me, Megan."

She sensed his reluctance to discuss the subject any further when he fell silent and drew her into his arms. He bowed his head and pressed his lips to her forehead. Her hands crept around his waist as if they had a will of their own. Angling her head, Megan pressed her parted lips to the side of his neck and scorched his skin with a chain of hot little kisses.

She felt Josh's arms tighten, and she fitted herself as closely to him as possible. The muscled wall of his chest cushioned her full breasts. His granite-hard abdomen and ridge of aroused flesh pressed intimately against her.

She met his searching mouth with a burst of hunger that startled her. Clinging tightly to him, she indulged her senses with a breathless exploration that left her craving much more.

Josh's aroused state became even more apparent when he held her hips closer still. Rocking against him in a rhythmic sway, Megan gloried in the erotic sensations coursing through her.

Josh slid his hands beneath the hem of Megan's white cotton sweater. Shielded by the semidarkness of the rose garden, he molded the curves and hollows of her body with his hands and savored the warmth and suppleness of her skin. When he felt the shudder that rippled through her, he skimmed his fingers forward until he held the weight of her swollen breasts.

She moaned softly, digging her fingers into his shoulders. Her head fell back as he plucked at her silk-covered nipples with gentle fingertips. He hungered to press his lips against her sensitive, swollen flesh.

Realizing that things were getting out of hand, Josh silently cursed himself. He forced himself to release Megan and smooth her sweater back into place. He held her then as though she were the most fragile thing in the world.

Megan sighed shakily as she stood in the circle of his arms, and uttered a silent indictment against herself. Flustered, she tried to step away, but Josh seemed reluctant to release her.

"I'm sorry, love. This is hardly the time or place for what we were about to do."

She laughed weakly. "Talk about feeling foolish."

He eased back and smiled at her, his expression rueful. "How is it that you always find the humor in things?"

She grinned. "There's nothing even remotely funny about the condition of my body."

"Bona fide agony," he concurred with a rakish wink, then took a deep, steadying breath.

"I guess we'd better get back upstairs."

Josh shifted uncomfortably, certain that it would be a few minutes before he could face the world. "You go ahead."

Megan's eyes widened with sudden under-standing, and she giggled.

"You sound about five years old," he com-mented as he took her hand.

"That's what happens when you hang out with preschoolers."

They resumed their stroll through the rose garden, periodically grinning at each other, but by the time they stepped off the elevator at the fourth floor and saw the somber expressions on the faces of Megan's family, neither one felt like laughing.

Once again, they waited.

A nurse scurried into the waiting room thirty minutes later. She motioned for Paul and Kathy, who immediately followed her.

"When is this torture going to end?" Megan groaned as Josh held her and she pressed her forehead to his shoulder.

"Soon, love. Very soon. Just hang on."

He stroked her back, needing to protect and comfort her. Barely aware of the curious looks directed at them by her family, Josh glanced at the clock. Only five minutes had passed since the nurse had summoned Kathy and Paul.

Megan heard the sound of footsteps in the otherwise-silent hospital corridor. She turned in Josh's loose embrace, then gripped his hand and whispered a fervent prayer.

The doctor, who appeared as fatigued as the family after more than ten hours spent monitor-ing Carrie, stepped into the room. Paul ap-peared behind him, tears shining in his eyes and a wide smile on his face.

"Good news, folks. Carrie is conscious and completely aware of her surroundings. She'll stay in the hospital for a few days for observation and additional tests, but her prognosis is excellent."

Ecstatic, Megan hugged and kissed Josh with abandon. With his attention focused solely on the woman in his arms, he barely heard the laughter and exclamations of relief that filled the air and gave the waiting room a partylike atmosphere.

Josh released Megan and watched her embrace each member of her family. Smiling almost wistfully, he didn't notice her mother until she was standing directly in front of him.

"I want to thank you for the kindness you've shown my family today, Mr. Wyatt. It's apparent that my daughter values your friendship a great deal."

His smile slipped as he studied the older woman. He sensed an underlying message in her words. "Please call me Josh."

"And I'm Eleanor. I also want you to know that I trust my daughter's instincts where her friends are concerned."

"Megan's a very special person, Mrs. Montgomery. I would never intentionally hurt her or violate her trust."

She nodded, a thoughtful look on her face as she moved closer to Josh. Although startled by her actions, he felt both moved and appreciative of the maternal warmth conveyed by her quick hug.

"Charles would have been very proud of you too," she said with the same straightforward manner evident in Megan's personality. "I know I am."

He felt his cheeks flush. "Thank you."

"I trust you'll see Megan safely home tonight."

"Of course, Mrs. Montgomery."

"Sunday dinner is usually at two. You're always welcome to join us." She grinned, once again reminding Josh of Megan. "If you aren't accustomed to a crowd and lots of little ones running about, then I'd advise earplugs and shin guards."

Megan slipped into place beside Josh. "Is Mother giving you the third degree?"

Eleanor wagged a finger at her daughter. "Young lady, you might give me credit for a modicum of subtlety."

"Yes, Mother."

The older woman turned away, laughter lighting her faded hazel eyes and deepening the creases around her mouth.

Josh glanced at Megan, his voice slightly strained as he spoke. "You're fortunate. She's very nice."

Megan knew enough about his past to realize that Eleanor Montgomery and Josh's late mother were as different as night and day. "She is nice, isn't she?" Bending down over a chair, Megan grabbed her purse.

"Ready to head home?" Josh asked.

She smothered a yawn with a hand. "Absolutely. This has been an impossibly long day."

He chuckled and slipped an arm around her. As they walked to the elevator, Megan burrowed closer to him and allowed herself to pretend that he would always be there for her when she needed him.

Eleven

"Wake up, Megan. You're home."

She shifted her head and noticed that Josh stood beside the open passenger door of the car. Megan gave him an owlish look as she struggled to get her bearings. "What time is it?" she asked, fumbling for her purse.

"After eleven."

He drew her out of the car and led her up to the house. After opening the door, he dropped her keys into her hand and closed her fingers around them.

"Get yourself to bed," he admonished.

Bewildered, she shook herself free of the lethargy caused by fatigue and the stress of the day. "You're leaving?" she questioned, unable to conceal her disappointment.

"You've had a rough day, Megan. Get some rest. We'll talk tomorrow."

Other than the quick brush of his lips across

her forehead, he didn't touch her. He simply left her standing in the open doorway, a slender figure in a white sweater and white wool slacks silhouetted by the light from a small lamp just inside the door.

"You really don't want to stay?" she asked in a tremulous voice.

Josh paused at the bottom of the porch steps. Slowly turning around, he looked up at her, his gaze hungry and his hands clenched into fists at his sides. With her silken cloud of auburn hair framing her face and tumbling across her shoulders, Megan resembled a single lighted taper in a tunnel of darkness.

"Of course I want to stay," he said patiently, "but you're exhausted."

"Are you all right?" Megan persisted, even though she knew she should just shut up and let him leave. "You seem . . . preoccupied about something."

"I've got a lot on my mind."

She felt her heart tremble, because she assumed that he was referring to his plan to depart Maryville without a backward glance or a second thought.

"We haven't talked yet about what happened at Tyler's this morning. Perhaps now is—"

He shook his head. "We'll talk when you're rested."

Unnerved by his behavior, Megan nodded forlornly and watched him leave. "I love you," she whispered as he started the car and slowly drove out of the driveway. "I love you so much, Josh.

Why can't you see that? Why can't you let yourself love me back?"

Tears started to sting her eyes. Trembling with emotion and fatigue, she forced herself to go inside, automatically locking the front door and then trudging up the staircase to her private quarters.

She shed her clothing as she walked across her bedroom, the disappointment she felt like a knife embedded in her heart. Despite her best efforts, Megan's thoughts remained centered on Josh. She hugged her pillow and eventually drifted into a fitful sleep, her emotions tattered and her dreams haunted by the image of the hard-featured self-made man who possessed her love.

Josh placed his suitcases at the foot of the bed. Leaving the guest room, he wandered downstairs.

While his home in St. Louis was spacious, Stanton House was much larger. And felt even emptier, he realized as he settled into his grandfather's library with a snifter of brandy.

He absently paged through one of the journals he'd perused a few days earlier, but the restless energy he now felt prevented him from concentrating on the handwritten passages for more than a few minutes.

Sighing heavily, he closed the leatherbound journal and leaned back in his chair. Josh took another sip of brandy and pondered his decision to move into Stanton House for the remainder of his stay in Maryville.

Despite the loneliness gnawing at him as he sat in the semidarkness of the library, he knew he'd made the right decision. He no longer felt threatened by the wishes of his late grandfather or by the truths revealed in his private papers.

Once a spur that drove him forward, his past now reminded him of a graveyard filled with the skeletons of his pain and suspicion. He felt no need to frequent such an emotional wasteland any longer.

If anything, he felt overtaken by a sensation of weariness whenever he tried to cling to the past or use it as a foil against the kindness and warmth he'd experienced since arriving in Maryville. He now considered the past unnecessary baggage, an empty container that had housed and periodically protected his emotions.

Josh recalled Daniel Cheney's frequent comment: "Knowledge is power, son, but that power is only worthwhile when it helps you understand yourself and your world."

Daniel, he suspected, would have approved of Megan, perhaps even thought of her as a kindred spirit. Like him, she was persistent and compassionate. And like him, she penetrated every emotional defense mechanism Josh devised.

With words and deeds Megan continuously demonstrated the value of openness and trust. Guilty of probing for hidden motives in every potential relationship, whether professional or personal, Josh knew he'd spent a lifetime clinging to his belief that kindness was a ploy to take advantage of him.

Megan, who didn't have a phony bone in her body, reflected the very real and incredibly genuine kindness of the Maryville community as a whole. Although hardly naive enough to characterize every person in the town as perfect, he sensed that the good far outweighed the bad.

He also silently acknowledged Megan's role as the catalyst that prompted him to unearth the courage and ability he needed to forgive the sins of the past, even his own, and to reveal the single most vulnerable part of himself—his hunger for love.

His hunger for *her* love, he amended silently.

He shook his head in wonder as she filled his thoughts. He felt a less than subtle tremor of desire ripple through his body as he recalled the unrestrained quality of her passion. Like no other woman he'd ever known, she unconsciously seduced him on every possible level.

Her laughter entranced him, and her devotion to her family and friends stirred him almost as profoundly as the gentle stroking of her hands across his naked body or the whisper of her gentle kisses against his lips.

He would value acceptance by her family, but he knew that only Megan could answer the cry for love resonating deep inside his soul. She touched his heart in ways no one ever had, and as he tried to visualize what his life would be like without her, all he saw was a yawning black hole of emptiness staring back at him.

He sensed that he would never experience the

reassurance of shared worry, shared joy, or the shared telling of unremarkable everyday events, unless he proved himself worthy of Megan's love.

A fragile seedling of hope began to take root in his thoughts. Somehow, Josh promised himself, he would find a way to Megan's heart.

Suddenly restless, he abandoned his brandy, jumped to his feet, and strolled across the room to the windows on the far side of the library. Staring out into the night, he noticed that he had an unrestricted view of the back of Megan's home.

His gaze automatically traveled up to the second-story balcony. He spotted a hint of light visible through the open French doors.

Despite the late hour, Josh didn't hesitate.

He needed Megan. He needed her touch and her tenderness. He needed her understanding and gentle nature, now and in the future. And he desperately needed her love.

He made his way out the side entrance and followed the narrow path that snaked through a sprawling flower garden to the gazebo behind Megan's home. Searching for a route to the upper level of the house, he spotted a winding staircase that led to the balcony, and went up.

Standing over her in the near-darkness of her bedroom a few minutes later, Josh frowned as he noted the restlessness of Megan's sleep. When he heard her murmur his name in a distressed tone, he hastily shed his clothes, loosened the sheet twisted around her body, and slipped into bed beside her.

Drawing her into his arms, Josh molded her

naked body to his own. He inhaled sharply when he felt the searing heat of her skin and the instinctive thrust of her hips against his loins.

Breathing in and out, slowly, painfully, he experienced the torment of suppressing the desire clamoring within him to simply surge into her body and lose himself in the sultry promise of her passion. Instead, he held her close, buried his face in the lilac scent of her tumbled auburn mane, and gently stroked her back and hips with his hands.

She stirred against him once more, fanning flames of arousal throughout Josh's body.

"Josh."

He smiled, liking the dreamy sound of his name as it sneaked past her lips.

Snuggling against the warmth and hardness of Josh's hair-roughened body, Megan sighed and floated on the edge of consciousness.

Gentle fingertips found the delicate flesh at the top of her thighs, and a moan of pleasure escaped her. Then she heard a soft chuckle.

Megan stiffened, swiftly realizing that she wasn't drifting through yet another vivid dream of Josh. All vestiges of sleep vanished.

"Josh . . . ?"

"Recognized me, did you?" he teased.

"I'd recognize you anywhere," she admitted, her body tingling with an awareness that tied her nerves into knots.

"You left your door unlocked."

Covering a yawn with the back of her hand, she shook her head. "I don't think so."

"The balcony doors."

"You came up the back way?"

He nodded, amused by her disbelief.

"Not the smartest thing you've ever done. The circular staircase is very unstable. That's why there's a gate at the bottom."

"I wasn't feeling smart, just needy," he admitted on a light note.

Shoving her hair out of her face, she eased onto her back and studied his rugged features. "I was dreaming about you."

"I know."

"You do?"

"You said my name in your sleep. Twice."

She smiled and quipped, "Caught in the act."

"You didn't sound happy the first time, though."

Her smile faded, and she looked away. "I guess I was having a bad dream."

Josh smoothed his hand over the curve of her hip, across her abdomen, and then trailed his fingertips up to the taut buds of her ripe breasts. Her shiver of pleasure sent a starburst of glittering sensation cascading into his bloodstream.

Megan shivered yet again, her senses bursting to life like a thousand firecrackers with each seductive stroke of his fingertips. When he paused, she craved his touch even more. She suddenly realized that she would be hungry for him for the rest of her life. The realization sobered her, and she felt a chill sweep across her heart.

Josh brought his hand up to the side of her face. Cradling her cheek with his palm, he turned her head and gently forced her to look at him.

Still and watchful, she peered up at him. Haunting uncertainly shadowed her hazel eyes, making them seem more brown than green.

"Shouldn't I be here, Megan?"

Unwilling to have him leave her twice in one night, she rolled into him. Parting her legs, she captured him between her thighs and arched her back so that her breasts plumped against the hair-covered wall of his chest.

Josh clamped a hand over her hip, locking her in place against him. "Do you want me to leave, Megan?"

If he wanted an answer, she decided, then she would provide one. She shifted her hips in a seductive manner against his hard flesh. The slight flaring of his nostrils and the way his chin lifted a notch when he ground his teeth together revealed his quest for control and assured Megan that she'd made her point.

Once Josh's breathing settled into an easier pace, she asked, "Do you have the answer to your question now?"

"Wanton," he accused in a low voice that promised eventual and very sensual retribution. "I left earlier because I thought it was the right thing to do under the circumstances."

She nodded, his reminder of the temporary nature of what they shared completely unwelcome. She loved him, so she shoved reality aside.

Megan traced his hard features with her fingertips, memorizing the contours and textures for later recollection. Lingering after several quiet but increasingly breathless minutes at his mouth, she skimmed the sensual shape of his lips.

She watched his face all the while. Concern began to well inside her when she glimpsed a telltale hint of uneasiness in his expression. "What's wrong, Josh?"

He shook his head, the self-protective instincts inside him still vital enough to make denial automatic. Silently gathering her against his body, he caressed the line of her brow with his lips.

Megan stroked his shoulder before threading her fingers through his thick black hair. "Talk to me. I know something's bothering you."

He exhaled heavily. "How, Megan?"

"How do I know?" At his nod she said, "I know because I care."

He suddenly shifted their bodies so that he wound up flat on his back with Megan sprawled across his chest. Her long hair draped around their heads to form a sensuous auburn curtain that shut out the world.

Still clasping him between her clenched thighs, she felt the pulsing strength of his maleness with every shuddering breath he took.

Megan said nothing. She simply remained poised above him, patient, loving, and worried about the feelings he felt compelled to hide from her.

"I need you, Megan."

She smiled. "I think we need each other right now."

He took her face in his hands and brought her closer. "Love me, Megan," he insisted, raw emotion underlining each word. "Make me feel whole. Make me feel as though I really belong in your arms and in your bed."

She felt her heart splinter into a thousand shards the instant he voiced his ragged plea. In that split second Megan realized that denying Josh would be like denying herself oxygen.

She consciously set aside the anxiety she felt over his impending departure, even though she knew she would eventually pay a high price for loving him. For the moment she didn't care, not when his need was this profound, this wrenching.

Megan leaned forward and kissed him, a wealth of love and tenderness flowing from her lips to his. She felt Josh's hands tremble as he held her, and she knew that no one had ever needed or desired her more.

"I tried not to want you," he whispered raggedly. "I tried so hard to stay away from you, but I kept needing you, the way I need you now. It's almost as though you're inside me, Megan, and I can't find the strength or the desire to push you away."

Megan suddenly realized that he, too, would pay a high price when he abandoned her. Her heart broke for both of them as she dropped searing kisses across his forehead, against his closed eyes, along his high cheekbones, and down his hard cheeks.

She lingered at the edge of his mouth, the tip of her tongue like a tender rapier as she traced the seam of his lips from edge to edge, and then returned to trace and taste his mouth yet again.

She died a little each time she suppressed the three words she longed to say, but she knew he didn't want to hear them. Despite all that, Megan discovered that she could say "I love you" with her hands, her lips, and with the invitation of her gently rocking hips.

She felt the tender power of Josh's hands as he explored the curves and hollows of her body. Moaning when he probed the secret heat between her thighs with his fingertips, she sighed with relief when he abruptly rolled their bodies to one side, tucked her beneath him, and then hovered over her.

She sank her fingers into the dense hair covering his chest. The hard, jutting strength nested between her thighs made her insides tremble and swell with desire. She whispered breathlessly, "Inside me, Josh. Please be inside me now."

"Patience, love," he said a second before he swooped down and captured her lips.

She opened to him instantly, the desire pounding through her veins and inflaming her senses so overwhelming that she groaned low in her throat.

She tasted him, adoring the intimacy of his exploring, seducing tongue as it swept past her lips and into her mouth. She shuddered, the sensations induced by his fingers trailing down her torso until they were poised at the entrance of the dark moist heat of her body.

She cried out as he stroked and caressed her. A frantic delirium enveloped her, and an ever-expanding inferno of desire and love incinerated her senses until they felt like burning embers.

She felt consumed as she tumbled forward to the crest of a wrenching climax before slowly floating back to the safe haven of Josh's embrace. She held fast to him until she could breathe again, think again, and feel again.

Josh tenderly joined their bodies. He watched Megan's face as he slowly filled her, feeling the give of her snug, wet flesh and the dark torrent bathing him with scorching flames.

Gasping for air, he paused. He saw her tears and her tremulous smile, and he heard the groan of renewed pleasure that escaped her. Despite his desire to go slowly with her, to love her gently, he couldn't restrain the reckless force within him that set his lower body into motion. He drove into her, seeking completion and wanting the oneness that he sensed only Megan could give him.

"I didn't know it could be like this," he confessed, his voice rough with disbelief and passion. "There's something very nearly spiritual happening when our bodies are joined this way."

Suddenly very still, Megan grew pale and tense.

"What is it?" he asked as he gentled his thrusts and stroked her body. He didn't want to rush headlong to completion. Instead, he wanted to give her a slow, sensual exploration of shared pleasure.

She closed her eyes, but tears seeped through the veil of her lashes. "I love you with all my heart, Josh. I'll always love you."

He breathed her name, the sound a harsh croak. He felt shattered, completely stunned by her declaration; then he remembered that other women had said the same words to him, but only in the throes of passion and never in the cold light of day. Josh wanted to believe her, but he hesitated, old habits not completely abandoned despite his desire to be free of them.

Megan closed her eyes, his silence an unwelcome reminder of the reality she had cast aside for a moment. A sob shook her as more tears trailed down her temples and into her hair.

When she shifted unexpectedly, Josh felt the movement of her body right down to his last nerve. Leaning down, he claimed her mouth, his thrusting tongue matching the movement of his lower body as he frantically surged in and out of her. He drank in her soft cries, finding sustenance in them. He felt her nails score his shoulders and back, but he experienced no pain.

Josh kept hearing her words in his mind as he soared toward satisfaction. He desperately longed to believe that she meant them, that they were prompted by more than the passionate madness of the moment.

Their movements grew even more frenzied, a feverishly insane ride that surpassed reason and control. Megan stiffened suddenly. Her entire body seemed to convulse, and she came apart beneath and around him.

Josh followed her into oblivion. Thought abandoned, consciousness in tatters, he surrendered to the trembling sensations of her body.

Her entire body throbbed, sustaining the loving inferno they shared until Josh breathlessly collapsed on top of her. She held him, love and fear mingling in her heart as she listened to the fierce sound of his breathing and felt the onset of the loneliness that would soon be her constant companion.

Twelve

Megan shifted in Josh's arms and peered sleepily at the clock on the nightstand. Stunned by what she saw, she blinked, then groaned in frustration when she again read: 8:05 A.M.

Josh mumbled something and tugged her back against him. She pulled away, hastily freed herself from the sheet tangled around her legs, and scooted to the edge of the bed.

"Problem?" he asked, rubbing the stubble that covered his cheeks and chin as he rolled onto his back.

"I forgot to set the alarm." Glancing at him, she shoved her hair out of her face, then felt a smile slowly spread across her face. "You look like a pirate."

He arched an eyebrow, his blue eyes warming as his gaze skimmed her naked torso. "And you look like a pirate's bounty. Shall I kidnap you this morning?"

She reluctantly got to her feet. "Absolutely not. One of my teachers won't be in until noon, and I need to be downstairs in less than twenty minutes."

"We can save time and water if we shower together."

"Only," she warned, trying to look stern as she slapped the very capable hands snaking toward her, "if you keep your paws to yourself."

He grinned and caught her wrist before she could flee. "How about dinner out tonight? Just to two of us?"

"Sounds like a lovely idea, but I've got a city-council meeting later this afternoon. I might be running a little behind schedule if someone gets long-winded."

"Busy lady," he groused as he released her. "Just let me know if I need to take a number."

She smiled, leaned down, dropped a kiss on the end of his nose, and fled from his hands, but she paused in the bathroom doorway. "You don't strike me as a man with enough patience to stand even in a short line, so forget about taking a number. I'll simply keep my dance card open for you until you leave."

Megan turned and disappeared into the bathroom, the shock of what she'd just said hitting her along with the cold water spurting out of the shower head. She suddenly felt battered by reality and the pain that accompanied it, but she found the strength to remind herself that a little happiness was better than none at all.

Unfortunately, she didn't believe that particular lie.

Determined not to give away her emotional upset to anyone, especially Josh, Megan pasted a smile on her face and quickly washed. She flashed a smile at him—for practice, she told herself as she tried to duck around him when he stepped into the shower a few minutes later.

He caught her, kissing her into a state of witlessness that made her smile disappear and her heart ache. She clutched his shoulders, the hunger sweeping over her making her mouth avid under his. When he released her lips and muttered something about the perils of foreplay, she laughed shakily and eased free of his embrace.

After brushing her teeth and applying clear gloss to her lips, Megan felt her jaws ache from her fake smile. She gave her face a rest in the bedroom as she stepped into a pair of bright floral leggings, pulled a loose, thigh-length matching T-shirt over her head, and then stepped into a pair of turquoise moccasins.

Megan twisted her long hair into a loose knot atop her head. She thought the upswept style, which was Gibson girlish, suited her attempt at a bright-eyed, all-is-well-with-the-world facade, but the shadows lurking beneath her large eyes hinted at something quite different.

Megan reproduced her pleasant expression when Josh strolled into the bedroom, clad only in a pair of partially fastened trousers that revealed his granite-like midsection. The shocking-pink towel draped around his neck emphasized his fierce masculinity, she realized, instead of detracting from it.

She watched every move he made, fascinated anew by the power and fluidity of his muscular body when he lifted his arms, stretched, brought his arms down again, and then padded barefoot to the bureau to retrieve his watch and wallet. Megan held her breath, her weak smile turning into a grimace before she remembered to fill her burning lungs with air.

Josh sat down on the edge of the bed and tugged on his socks. He glanced in her direction, an almost boyish grin gentling the harsh contours of his face. "I've moved up my return flight to St. Louis, so I'll be leaving tomorrow."

She froze as his words penetrated her dazed brain. Her smile faded, and she backed up, her eyes fixed on his relaxed expression as she fumbled for the doorknob.

On the verge of suffocating, she tugged open the door. Megan and Josh instantly heard high-pitched giggling and the slamming of the front door, a sign that several preschoolers had arrived for the day.

"Josh, I . . ."

He smiled at her. "I understand. Duty calls. I'll see you tonight. There are a lot of things I need to tell you. We fell asleep before we could talk last night. Why don't I pick you up around six?"

She nodded, amazed that he could be so casual while her heart thudded in her chest. She tried to speak, but her throat closed up on her, so she nodded again and backed gracelessly out the door.

Little feet pounded up the oak stairs, forcing her to release her grip on the knob. She turned, dredged up another smile, and faced the mini-horde that had come in search of her.

Megan ran out of smiles and decided to quit pretending that she felt wonderful shortly after lunch, a direct result of a typical morning of preschool madness and an attempted inquisition regarding Josh by two of her sisters, who'd dragged their mother along for the ride.

Megan silently blessed her mother when the older woman immediately noticed the distress in her daughter's eyes. Eleanor Montgomery promptly directed Megan's sisters to cease and desist immediately, and after herding them out the front door, she paused to gently remind Megan, "If you need a shoulder, you can call me."

On the verge of sobbing, Megan simply nodded.

"Is it Josh, sweetheart?"

"Yes," she choked out.

"It's obvious he cares about you, Megan."

"But not enough, Mom. Just not enough."

"Would you like to spend the evening at home with me? Your dad's got his Bassmaster's Club meeting after supper, so it would be only the two of us."

She shook her head. "Thanks, but I need to work this through on my own."

"You've always done that, haven't you?" Eleanor questioned gently as she hugged Megan. "Sometimes being alone isn't the answer, but I won't push you. Just know that I'm nearby if you need me."

Once the family departed and she had a full preschool staff in place once again, Megan excused herself and retreated to the upstairs library in search of privacy.

She bypassed lunch in favor of aspirin for the miserable throbbing in her head, the result, she supposed, of watching her dream of finding happiness with the right man go up in smoke right before her eyes.

She sagged into her favorite chair, parked her feet on a hassock, and closed her eyes while she massaged her temples. She dozed off almost immediately, but she dreamed of the intimate moments she'd shared with Josh.

After freshening up and changing into attire suitable for a city-council meeting, Megan arrived at the city-hall meeting room in time to chair the zoning board's presentation of plans for a new community center in a low-income Maryville neighborhood. Funded by a grant established several years earlier by Charles Stanton, the community center was of special concern to Megan because of her role as the estate's executor.

The council voted to approve the community center following Megan's detailed remarks. She thanked the members of the city council for their unanimous support and returned to her seat. Her footsteps faltered when she spotted Josh walking up the center aisle of the meeting room.

She slipped into her chair, feeling uncertainty

when the mayor announced, "Ladies and gentlemen, our final speaker this afternoon will be Joshua Wyatt, who has asked for an opportunity to address this open city-council meeting."

Megan nervously picked a piece of lint from the skirt of her knit dress as she watched Josh take his place at the podium. She now understood the reason for the unusual standing-room- only crowd that evening, and she credited Maryville's rumor mill with accomplishing what the city fathers never could.

Attired in a tailored charcoal-gray business suit, Josh radiated confidence. Sighing softly, Megan fought the urge to flee. She stayed put, praying that she appeared composed as she studied Josh's strikingly rugged features.

Looking out at the sea of faces smiling back at him and listening to the applause of the citizens of Maryville, Josh felt even more certain about the decisions he'd made in recent days. Having reached a crossroads in his life, he knew that the new route he'd selected for the future held potential for both personal happiness and new professional challenges.

He glanced at Megan, frowning slightly when he noticed the panic in her eyes before she looked away. Although he longed to reassure her that everything was all right, he didn't have the privacy he needed to do so.

"Mr. Wyatt?" the mayor prompted encouragingly.

"Thank you, Mr. Mayor."

Relaxed and assured, Josh placed his hands on either side of the top of the podium and addressed the crowd. "First of all, I'd like to express my sincere thanks to all of you for the hospitality I've enjoyed since arriving in Maryville. Many of you have taken the time to speak with me privately and to share your thoughts about Charles Stanton, especially since you know that I didn't have an opportunity to meet him prior to his death. He and I both share responsibility for that oversight, I'm afraid."

He paused for a moment before admitting, "When I was first notified of Mr. Stanton's death, I resisted the idea of even coming here. I had no real interest in his estate or in stirring up memories of my own past, which I felt were best left buried and forgotten. To be perfectly candid, I also didn't care about the wishes or the motives or the wealth of a man I'd learned to hate during my childhood, but the persistent efforts and the patience of Charles Stanton's attorney and his executor forced me to confront my heritage, my inheritance, and some personal demons that have plagued me for years."

The audience buzzed with dismay, but they quieted when Josh raised his hands.

"I came here grudgingly and with a big chip on my shoulder," he confessed. "Because I felt threatened, I was angry and defensive and filled with resentment, so much so that I nearly overlooked the most valuable aspect of my inheritance. One person in particular helped remind me that the past is important, especially if we're in danger of repeating the mistakes of those who came before us."

Pausing, he scanned the room. Josh felt reassured by the compassion and concern he glimpsed in the faces of the townspeople. He saw only shock when he looked at Megan.

"I've spent several days wrestling with both the past and the present. My reluctance to trust people is a habit I acquired during a childhood that lacked the warmth and affection that seems so commonplace among the people I've met here."

Josh said laughingly, "I'm still getting used to how genuinely nice you all are. Anyway, for most of my life I've felt . . ." He hesitated, searching for the right word ". . . hollow inside. Perhaps incomplete is an even better description, but I don't feel that way any longer. Despite my success in the travel industry, my private life has been almost nonexistent. I've also been lonely, because I've avoided close friendships."

"Through reading his private papers and in talking to many of you, I've discovered that my . . . my grandfather was a proud and stubborn man. Unfortunately, I share those same qualities with him, but I'm working on overcoming them." He smiled at the audience, disarming and thoroughly charming them with his candor and the self-deprecating humor glowing in his blue eyes.

"Quite frankly, I feel as though I've been seduced by an entire town. I no longer intend to abandon my heritage or reject my inheritance, although I admit that I came to Maryville with every intention of doing exactly that. I plan to make Maryville my home, and intend to carry on my grandfather's commitment to the people who live and work here. I won't give up Cheney-Wyatt, but I'll oversee, with the able assistance of the current personnel, the various businesses founded by the Stanton family. In doing that, I know that I'll finally become a part of something far more important than myself."

Josh felt invigorated by his own honesty. "In conclusion, I want you to know that I've formally accepted the Stanton estate with the assistance of Mr. Dunwoody, and my one hope as we face the future together is that I will eventually earn the respect you all gave to my late grandfather, Charles Stanton."

Nearly deafened by the applause that exploded in the meeting hall, Megan watched in amazement as people converged on Josh. Everyone spoke at once. He received more pats on the back and shook more hands than a politician stumping the election circuit.

I've succeeded, she thought dazedly. I've actually managed to keep my promise to Charles, so why do I suddenly feel like a soft drink that's gone flat?

Megan seized her briefcase, left her chair, and began the arduous process of easing her way through the enthusiastic throng of well-wishers. She glanced back at Josh only once. Relieved that he seemed too busy to notice her retreat, she swiftly left the meeting hall.

She needed time, Megan told herself during the short drive home. Time to come to terms with her shock at Josh's about-face regarding his inheritance, and time to deal with the personal price she'd paid for keeping her promise to Charles Stanton.

She ground her teeth together to prevent herself from wailing like a wounded animal, but she couldn't stop the tears that started to fall from her eyes. Given Josh's plan to make Maryville his home, she would be reminded of her foolishness every time they encountered each other, which, she realized, would be often. Far too often. Probably daily, since they were destined, it seemed, to become neighbors.

Quietly cursing the recklessness with which she'd given him her love, she marched into her house. After assuring herself that no one had lingered in the lower level, Megan locked the front door and went upstairs to her bedroom. She exchanged her dress and heels for the comfort of a caftan before making her way back down to the gazebo behind the house.

She sat there alone for more than an hour, watching as the sun slipped beneath the horizon. Megan felt sheltered by the darkness and the sweet, heavy scent of the blossoming roses that nearly encircled the tiny structure, but the serenity of the environment didn't lessen the dull ache in her heart or the melancholy feelings sweeping over her.

No longer comforted by the consuming darkness, she found matches on a nearby table, put a flame to the wick of a single candle, and was immediately reminded of the first meal she had shared with Josh.

"I love him, but he doesn't believe in love," she

whispered to herself. He'd told her, but, like a fool, she'd ignored his warning.

Megan sighed, frustrated by her own stupidity. Leaning forward, she drew her legs up, pressed her forehead to her knees, and waited for the pain to recede. It didn't. She doubted that it ever would.

She heard footsteps the instant before Josh stepped into the gazebo. Brushing at her cheeks, she straightened and tried to appear calm and cheerful. Certain of failure, she quickly dropped "cheerful" from her mental list.

"What's going on, Megan? Your house is locked up tighter than Fort Knox."

"Nothing's going on," she insisted. "I was just relaxing. I've had a long day."

He sat down beside her on the cushioned bench and smiled at her. "This is a nice change from the council meeting. You disappeared, and then it took me more than an hour to get out of there."

Megan said nothing. She knew that if she uttered a single word, she would sound mean-spirited.

"I'll never be able to repay you for what you've done, Megan."

Determined to appear nonchalant, she shrugged. "The estate pays my expenses, so you won't be getting a bill."

Startled by her flip comment, he studied her. "That's not what I meant."

"What do you mean, Josh?"

"I meant that even though I resented being

manipulated into making the trip down here, you nudged me just hard enough and provoked my curiosity to such a degree that I wound up asking myself some really tough questions, questions I've avoided for many years. I also confronted some less than wonderful truths about myself."

"Well, I'm glad I could help, especially since you've obviously found all the answers," she managed to say briskly. She was so close to tears that she fought the urge to jump to her feet and run out of the gazebo. Instead, she got up slowly and observed, "I guess we'll be neighbors fairly soon."

"I hoped we'd be living together," he admitted, his gaze narrowing as she inched farther and farther away from him.

"I couldn't do that. I have a reputation to consider, Josh. People trust me with their very young and very impressionable children." Aware of the strident tone in her voice, she forced herself to settle down. "What would they think if I became your live-in lover? This is a small town, after all."

"Live-in lover?" he repeated quietly.

She kept edging away, determined to get as far from him as she could.

He moved quickly and without warning, just like the predator she'd compared him to during their first moments together. "Why are you acting this way?"

She tried to jerk free of him, but he simply tightened his grip on her wrist.

"Megan, you're running away from me. Tell

me why!" he barked, his anger and frustration rising to the surface. "Didn't you hear anything I said at the council meeting?"

"Oh, yes, I heard every single word. You're quite an articulate man, Josh."

He grabbed her shoulders and shook her. "What's gotten into you? Answer me, dammit!"

She held still, waited for him to calm down, and then said in the softest voice he'd ever heard, "Take your hands off me."

Shocked by his own behavior, he did so, instantly. She tore out of the gazebo and raced through the dark. Shoving open the kitchen door and just barely holding back her tears, she tried to slam the door shut.

Josh burst inside. Megan jumped back as the door bounced against the wall at least half a dozen times. She opened her mouth to speak, but she felt too flustered to say anything.

"Don't say a word. I'll pay the repair bills if I've damaged anything."

"Leave me alone, Josh. Please leave me alone."

"Not on a bet."

Burgeoning tears made her throat swell, and she choked out, "I can't do this anymore."

"You can't do *what* anymore?" he demanded, his chest rapidly rising and falling as he towered over her.

"I can't pretend."

Josh went as still as stone. All the color seemed to drain from his face. Mastering his emotions, he said, "You don't need to run away from me. Just talk to me, and try to make sense this time. What exactly do you mean by pretending?"

She glared at him, unwilling to reveal the true depths of her own stupidity. "There's every need to run away. I keep falling into bed with you. I don't want to be used." She stopped trying not to cry. "I can't . . . I can't . . . I can't talk about this," she gasped.

He grabbed her before she could turn and dart out of the kitchen. He felt helpless in the face of the emotions ravaging her, but he finally understood them.

"I've been a fool," he whispered hoarsely. "A total fool."

"I'm the fool," she cried. Wilting against his strong body, she sobbed so brokenly that he uttered an oath of pure self-recrimination.

"Megan?"

She finally lifted her wet face.

"I assumed you knew."

"Knew what?" she asked, her voice a shattered mess.

"That I'm in love with you. That nothing, not all the money or the prestige or the power that goes with being a Stanton, means anything if you aren't a part of my life."

Her chin wobbled and then turned stubborn. "I won't be your live-in lover. I deserve better than that."

Josh promptly lost patience. Without another word he hauled her up into his arms, exited her house, stalked down the long path that connected the two mansions, and then carried her through the side entrance of Stanton House. Making his way up the stairs, he strode down the carpeted hallway and into a bedroom, where he dumped her on the bed.

Furious with his high-handed behavior, Megan pulled herself up to her knees, her expression stormy.

"Look around," he commanded.

She did, grudgingly, and knew her eyes slowly widened when she noticed clear signs of masculine occupation. The open closet door revealed some of the clothes he'd worn since his arrival. The keys to Stanton House rested atop the bureau. His leather deck shoes had been kicked off just inside the bathroom door. Even the scent of his sophisticated cologne lingered in the air.

"You've moved in," she breathed in surprise.

He nodded, but he made no move to approach her. Instead, he stood in the center of the room, clearly the master of his new home. "I'm not in the market for a live-in lover. I want a wife, children eventually, and a real home. You are at the heart of the entire plan. Without you the rest of the plan won't work. Without your love I'll never be whole."

She got to her feet on the bed, staggering as she walked across the mattress. "Was that a proposal?" she asked.

He nodded, but he waited for her to move closer before he answered, "It was."

She flung herself into his arms. "I accept!" she cried before peppering his face with a dozen hot little kisses.

"Do you promise to always love me?" Josh asked, the vulnerability he'd long felt no longer hidden from Megan.

She smiled gently. "I promise, and you already know that I always keep my promises."

THE EDITOR'S CORNER

Next month LOVESWEPT celebrates heroes, those irresistible men who sweep us off our feet, who tantalize us with whispered endearments, and who challenge us with their teasing humor and hidden vulnerability. Whether they're sexy roughnecks or dashing sophisticates, dark and dangerous or blond and brash, these men are heartthrobs, the kind no woman can get enough of. And you can feast your eyes on six of them as they alone grace each of our truly special covers next month. HEARTTHROBS—heroes who'll leave you spellbound as only real men can.

Who better to lead our HEARTTHROBS lineup than Fayrene Preston and her hero, Max Hayden, in **A MAGNIFICENT AFFAIR**, LOVESWEPT #528? Max is the best kind of kisser: a man who takes his time and takes a woman's breath away. And when Ashley Whitfield crashes her car into his seaside inn, he senses she's one sweet temptation he could go on kissing forever. But Ashley has made a habit of drifting through her life, and it'll take all of Max's best moves to keep her in his arms for good. A magnificent love story, by one of the best in the genre.

The utterly delightful **CALL ME SIN**, LOVESWEPT #529, by award-winner Jan Hudson, will have you going wild over Ross Berringer, a Texas Ranger as long and as tall as his twin brother, Holt, who thrilled readers in **BIG AND BRIGHT**, LOVESWEPT #464. The fun in **CALL ME SIN** begins when handsome hunk Ross moves in next door to Susan Sinclair, the prim bookstore owner has been missing in her life—and the perfect partner to help her track down a con artist. But once Ross's downright neighborly attention turns Susan inside out with ecstasy, she starts running scared. How Ross unravels her intriguing mix of passion and fear is a sinfully delicious story you'll want to read.

Doris Parmett outdoes herself in creating a perfect HEARTTHROB in **MR. PERFECT**, LOVESWEPT #530. Chase Rayburn is the epitome of sex appeal, a confirmed bachelor who can charm a lady's socks off—and then all the rest of her clothes. So why does he feel wildly jealous over Sloan McKay's personal ad on a billboard? He's always been close to his law partner's widow and young son, but he's never before wanted to kiss Sloan until she melted with wanton pleasure. Shocking desire, daring seduction, and a friendship that deepens into love—a breathtaking combination in one terrific book.

Dangerously sexy, his gaze full of delicious promises, Hunter Kincaid will have you dreaming of **LOVE AND A BLUE-EYED COWBOY,** LOVESWEPT #531, by Sandra Chastain. Hunter knows he can win the top prize in a motorcycle scavenger hunt, but he doesn't count on being partnered with petite, smart-mouthed Fortune Dagosta. A past sorrow has hardened Hunter's heart, and the last person he wants for a companion for a week is a beautiful woman whose compassion is easily aroused and whose body is made for loving. Humorous and poignant, the sensual adventure that follows is a real winner!

Imagine a man who has muscles like boulders and a smoky drawl that conjures up images of rumpled sheets and long, deep kisses—that's Storm Dalton, Tami Hoag's hero in **TAKEN BY STORM,** LOVESWEPT #532. A man like that gets what he wants, and what he wants is Julia McCarver. But he's broken her heart more than once, and she has no intention of giving him another chance. Years of being a winning quarterback has taught Storm ways to claim victory, and the way he courts Julia is a thrilling and funny romance that'll keep you turning the pages.

Please give a rousing welcome to new author Linda Warren and her first LOVESWEPT, **BRANDED,** #532, a vibrantly emotional romance that has for a hero one of the most virile rodeo cowboys ever. Tanner Danielson has one rule in life: Never touch another man's wife. And though he wanted Julie Fielding from the first time he saw her, he never tasted her fire because she belonged to another. But now she's free and he isn't waiting a moment longer. A breathlessly exciting love story with all the wonderfully evocative writing that Linda displayed in her previous romances.

On sale this month from FANFARE are three marvelous novels. **LIGHTS ALONG THE SHORE,** by immensely talented first-time author Diane Austell, is set in nineteenth-century California, and as the dramatic events of that fascinating period unfold, beautiful, impetuous Marin Gentry must face up to the challenges in her turbulent life, including tangling with notorious Vail Severance. Highly acclaimed Patricia Potter delivers **LAWLESS,** a poignant historical romance about a schoolteacher who longs for passionate love and finds her dreams answered by a coldhearted gunfighter who's been hired to drive her off her land. In **HIGHLAND REBEL,** beloved author Stephanie Bartlett whisks you away to the rolling hills and misty valleys of the Isle of Skye, where proud highland beauty Catriona Galbraith is fighting for her land and her people, and where bold Texas rancher Ian MacLeod has sworn to win her love.

Also available this month in the hardcover edition from Doubleday (and in paperback from FANFARE in March) is **LUCKY'S LADY** by ever-popular LOVESWEPT author Tami Hoag. Those of you who were enthralled with the Cajun rogue Remy Doucet in **THE RESTLESS HEART,** LOVESWEPT #458, will find yourself saying Ooh la la when you meet his brother, Lucky, for he is one rough and rugged man of the bayou. And when he takes the elegent Serena Sheridan through a Louisiana swamp to find her grandfather, they generate what *Romantic Times* has described as "enough steam heat to fog up any reader's glasses."

Happy reading!

With warmest wishes,

Nita Taublib

Nita Taublib
Associate Publisher/LOVESWEPT
Publishing Associate/FANFARE

Every woman dreams of getting LUCKY. . . .

When Serena Sheridan gets lucky, she gets *Lucky Doucet,*

the sizzling, bad-boy Cajun hero of

Tami Hoag's

LUCKY'S LADY

On sale in hardcover in late January from Doubleday and from FANFARE in the spring, and

already winning rave reviews from <u>Romantic Times</u> and <u>Rendezvous</u>:

FN 25 - 2/92

FANFARE

Now On Sale

LIGHTS ALONG THE SHORE

(29331-1) $5.99/6.99 in Canada

by Diane Austell

*Marin Gentry has proven that she is woman to be reckoned with -- but
she is also a woman who must finally admit how she longs to be loved.
A completely involving and satisfying novel,
and the debut of a major storyteller.*

LAWLESS

(29071-1) $4.99/5.99 in Canada

by Patricia Potter

author of RAINBOW

*Willow Taylor holds within her heart a love of the open frontier -- and a
passion for a renegade gunman they call Lobo -- the lone wolf.
Their hearts run free in a land that is LAWLESS. . . .*

HIGHLAND REBEL

(29836-5) $4.99/5.99 in Canada

by Stephanie Bartlett

author of HIGHLAND JADE

*Catriona Galbraith is a proud Highland beauty consumed with the fight to
save the lush rolling hills of her beloved home, the Isle of Skye. Ian
MacLeod is the bold American sworn to win her love.*

FANFARE

On Sale in February

New York Times Bestseller
TEXAS! SAGE
☐ (29500-4) $4.99/5.99 in Canada
by Sandra Brown

The third and final book in Sandra Brown's beloved TEXAS! trilogy. Sage Tyler always thought she wanted a predictable, safe man . . . until a lean, blue-eyed drifter took her breath, and then her heart away.

SONG OF THE WOLF
☐ (29014-2) $4.99?5.99 in Canada
by Rosanne Bittner

Young, proud, and beautiful, Medicine Wolf possesses extraordinary healing powers and a unique sensitivity that leads her on an unforgettable odyssey into a primeval world of wildness, mystery, and passion.

LATE NIGHT DANCING
☐ (29557-8) $5.99/6.99 in Canada
by Diana Silber

A compelling novel of three friends -- sophisticated Los Angeles women with busy, purposeful lives, who also live on the fast track of romance and sex, because, like lonely women everywhere, they hunger for a man to love.

SUMMER'S KNIGHT
☐ (29549-7) $4.50/5.50 in Canada
by Virginia Lynn

Heiress Summer St. Clair is stranded penniless on the streets of London. But her terrifying ordeal soon turns to adventure when she captures the glittering eyes of the daring Highland rogue, Jamie Cameron.

☐ Please send me the books I have checked above. I am enclosing $ _____ (add $2.50 to cover postage and handling). Send check or money order, no cash or C. O. D.'s please.

Mr./ Ms. _____

Address _____

City/ State/ Zip _____

Send order to: Bantam Books, Dept. FN, 414 East Golf Road, Des Plaines, IL 60016

Please allow four to six weeks for delivery.

Prices and availability subject to change without notice.

THE SYMBOL OF GREAT WOMEN'S FICTION FROM BANTAM

Ask for these books at your local bookstore or use this page to order.

FN23 - 2/92

"A delightfully refreshing amalgam of Regency
Romance set during a parallel to the French Revolution
with elements of magic thrown in. . . . A most
impressive accomplishment."
--Katherine Kurtz, author of the
DERYNI CHRONICLES

ILLUSION

by Paula Volsky

In a world where magic determines birthright, spoiled
nobleman's daughter Eliste vo Derrivale hopes to be
presented to the king at the dazzling court in Sherreen.
She leaves behind her love for a man whom by law she
can never marry, and takes the chance to pursue her
dream -- a dream abruptly shattered by the violent
revolution that tears her world apart. It's a rebellion that
could bring her the love she desires. But first, like the
peasants she disdained, she must scramble for bread in
the streets of the city, orphaned and outlawed by the new
regime. At the height of her despair, she finds the man
she long ago left behind and together, in a country
wracked with change, they must find a way to survive in
a world gone mad . . . with liberty.

Magic: it's pure illusion.
ILLUSION:
it's pure magic!

On sale now in hardcover and trade paperback
wherever Bantam Spectra books are sold.

AN 398--2/92